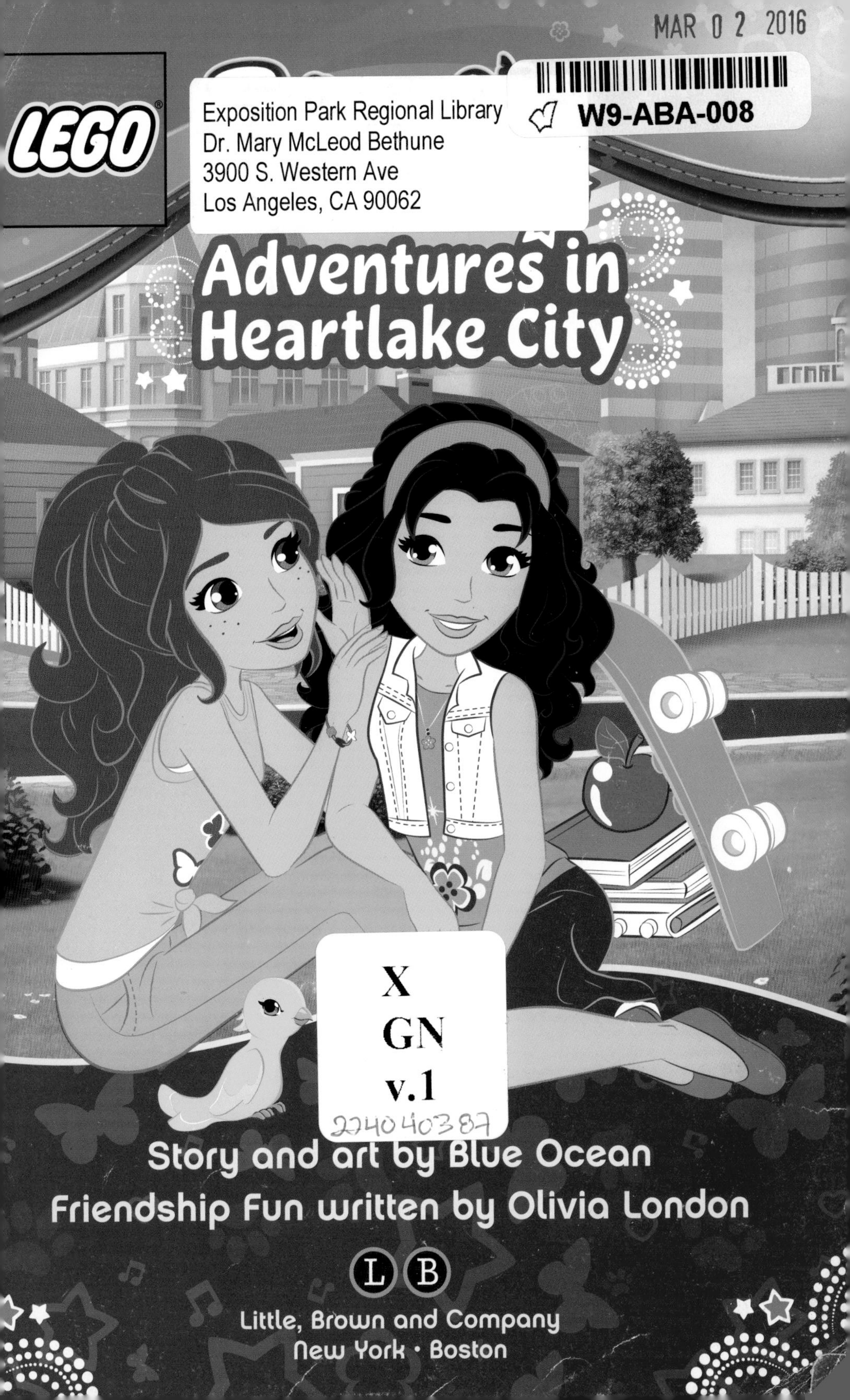

LEGO
Adventures in Heartlake City
Story and art by Blue Ocean
Friendship Fun written by Olivia London
LB
Little, Brown and Company
New York · Boston

Little, Brown and Company

Hachette Book Group
1290 Avenue of the Americas, New York, NY 10104
Visit us at lb-kids.com

Little, Brown and Company is a division of Hachette Book Group, Inc. The Little, Brown name and logo are trademarks of Hachette Book Group, Inc.

The publisher is not responsible for websites (or their content) that are not owned by the publisher.

First Edition: October 2015

Library of Congress Control Number: 2015945451

Paperback ISBN: 978-0-316-26614-7
Paper over Board ISBN: 978-0-316-30918-9

10 9 8 7 6 5 4 3 2 1

LAKE

Printed in the United States of America

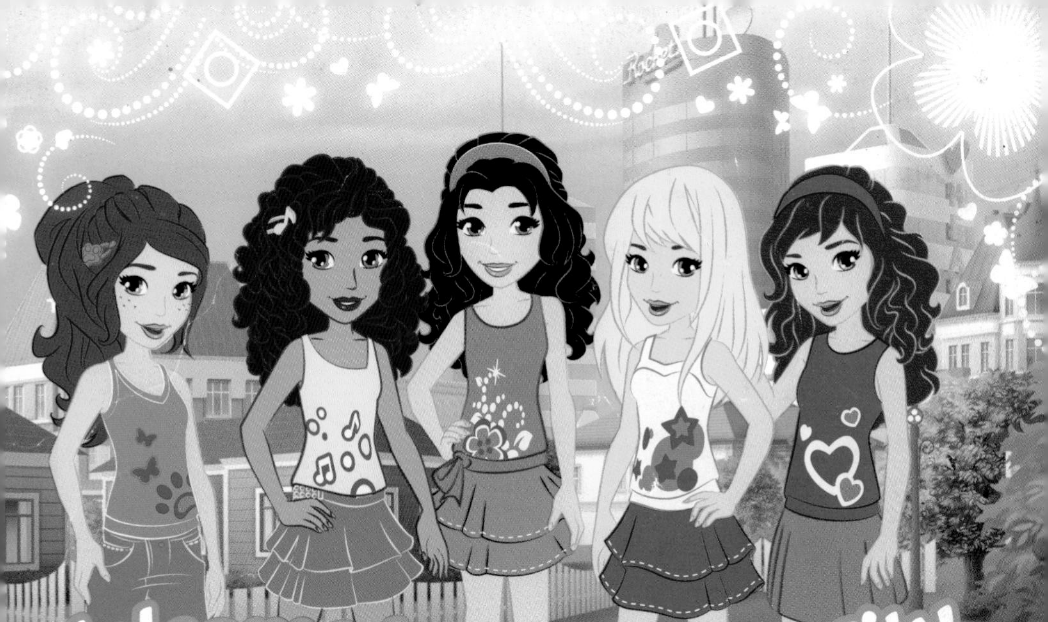

Welcome to Heartlake City

Heartlake City is the home of LEGO Friends, five very different and very talented girls who are best friends. The city is centered around a heart-shaped lake (hence the name!), located directly between a beach and a mountain range. This location makes it perfect for all kinds of outdoor activities like flying, horse riding, dolphin observing, and more! The city itself is home to a mall, a café, a bakery, a vet, a beauty shop, a swimming pool, and adventure!

Great Places to Visit!

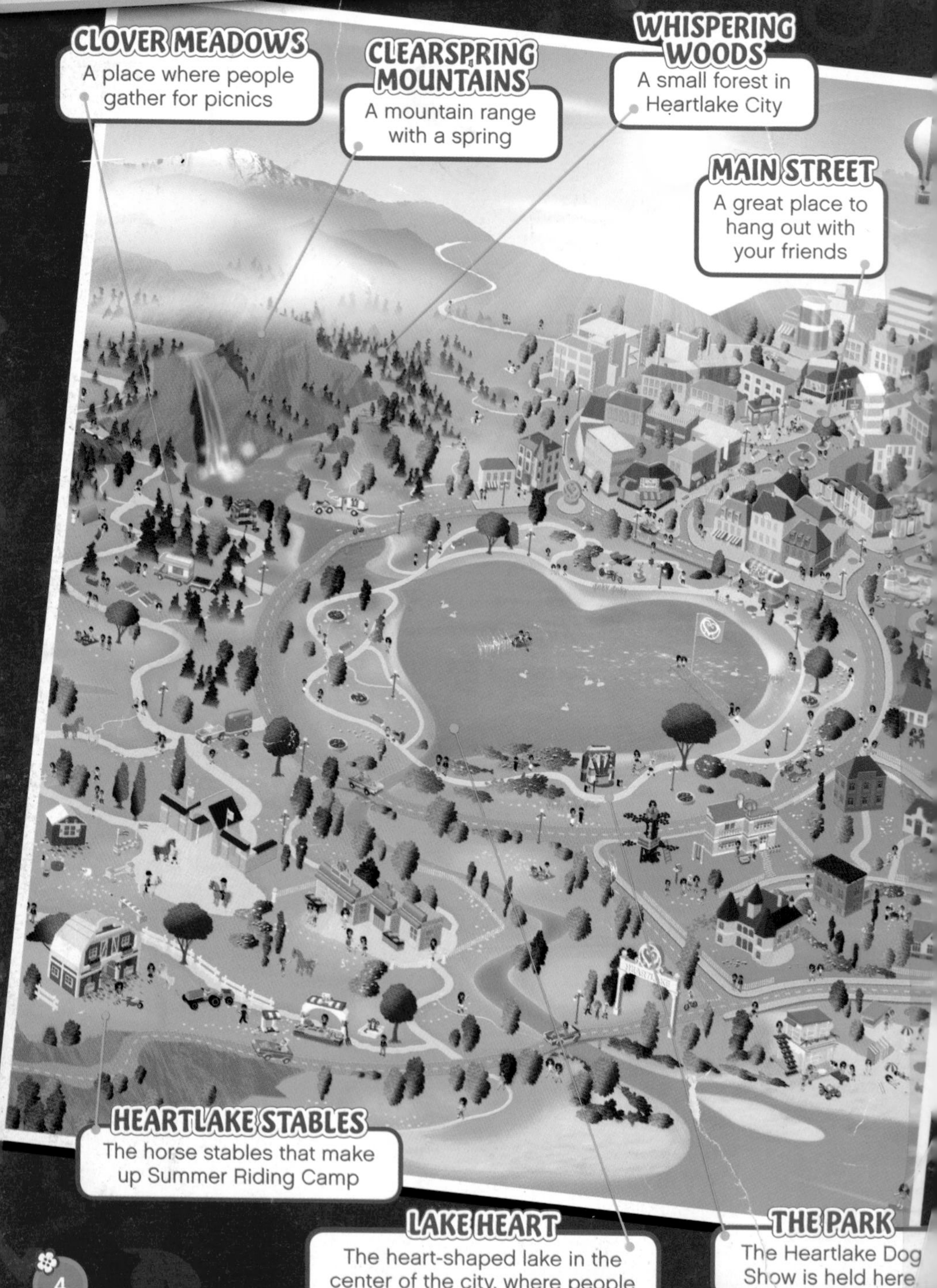

CLOVER MEADOWS
A place where people gather for picnics
CLEARSPRING MOUNTAINS
A mountain range with a spring
WHISPERING WOODS
A small forest in Heartlake City
MAIN STREET
A great place to hang out with your friends
HEARTLAKE STABLES
The horse stables that make up Summer Riding Camp
LAKE HEART
The heart-shaped lake in the center of the city, where people go to swim, fish, and ice skate
THE PARK
The Heartlake Dog Show is held here.

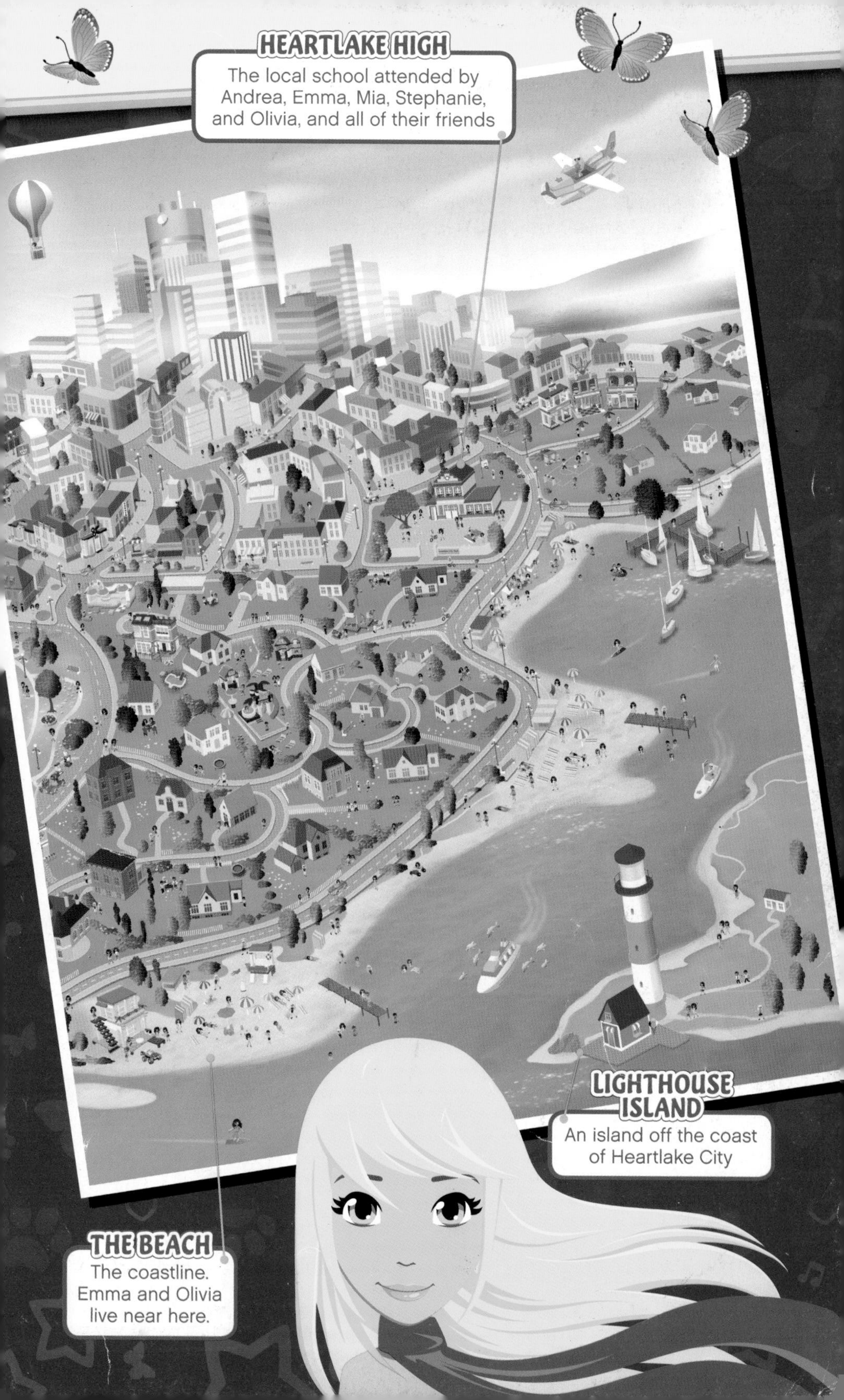
HEARTLAKE HIGH
The local school attended by Andrea, Emma, Mia, Stephanie, and Olivia, and all of their friends
LIGHTHOUSE ISLAND
An island off the coast of Heartlake City
THE BEACH
The coastline. Emma and Olivia live near here.

Andrea

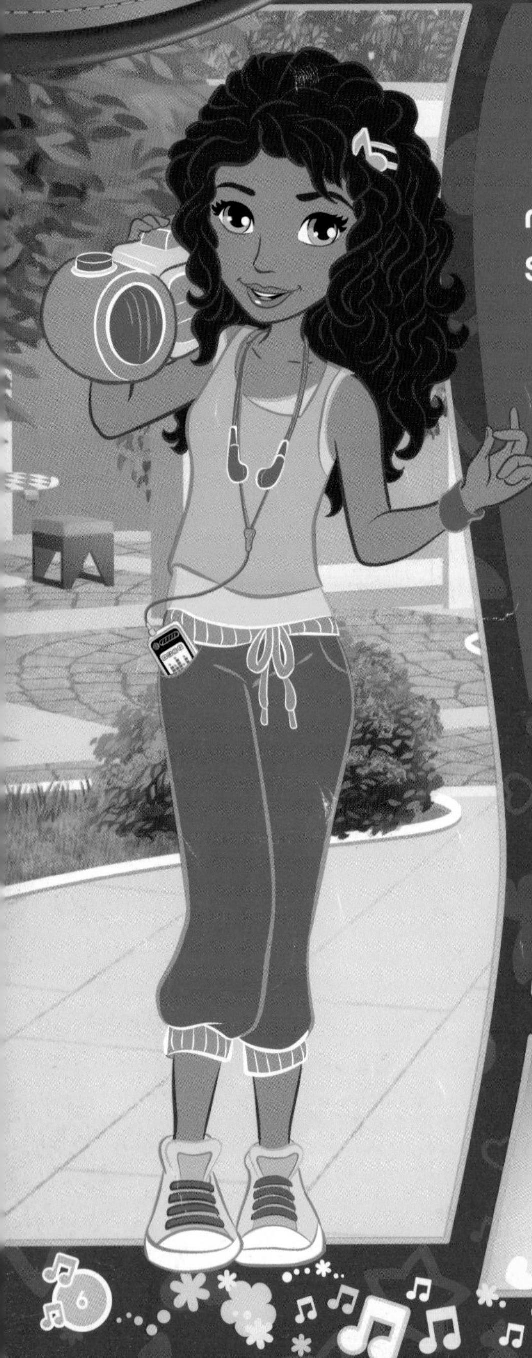

The musician of the group, Andrea is a talented singer and is great at making up her own songs. She loves anything that pertains to music: singing, playing the piano, dancing, and the theater. But she is a great cook and works at a café. She also has a not-so-secret love of bunnies.

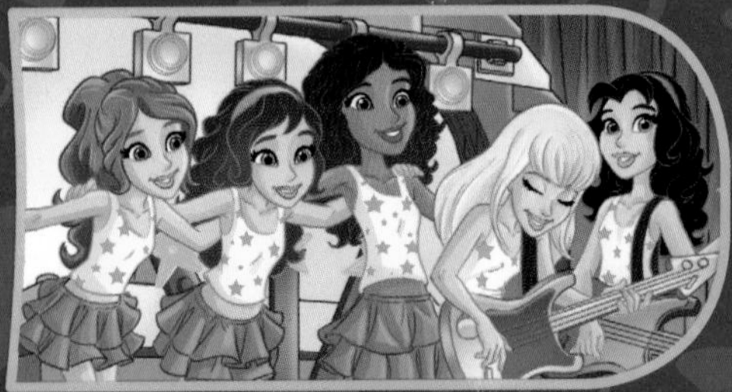

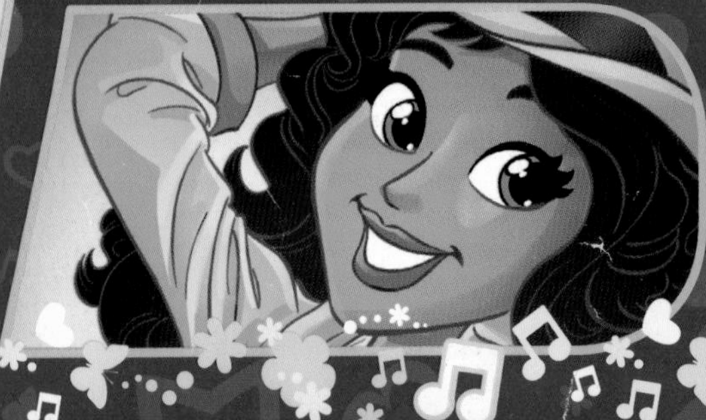

Emma

Emma is a very trendy girl who loves style. Definitely the fashionista of the group, she enjoys fashion design, making jewelry, interior design, and makeovers. She's also a fan of English horseback jumping and karate. She is sometimes forgetful and unable to speak up for herself, but she's a wonderful friend.

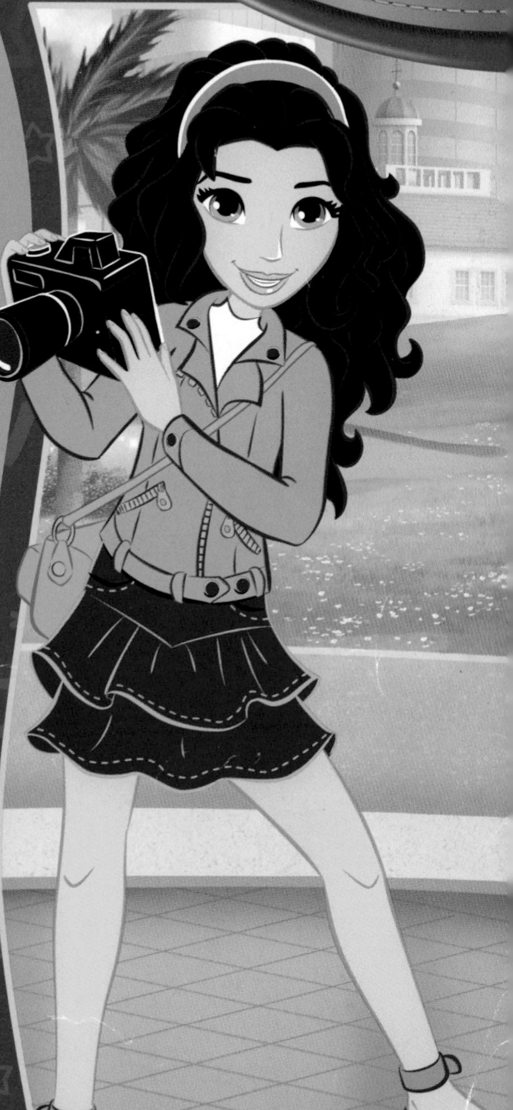

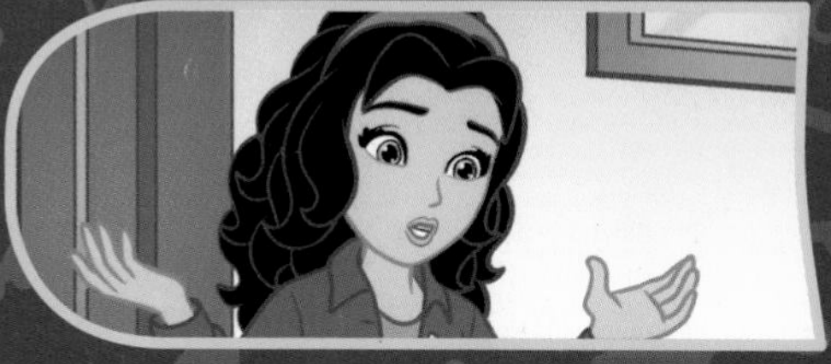

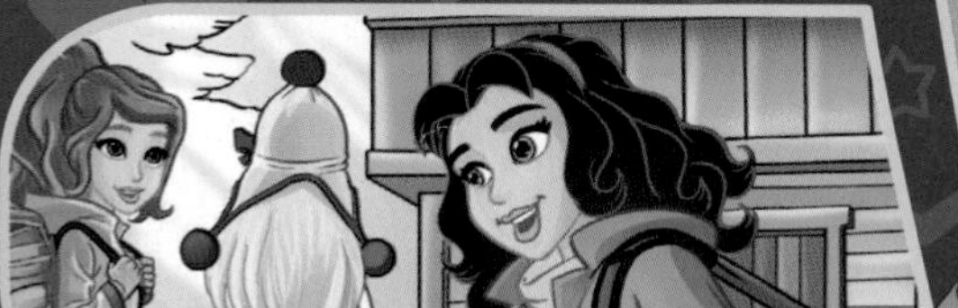

Mia

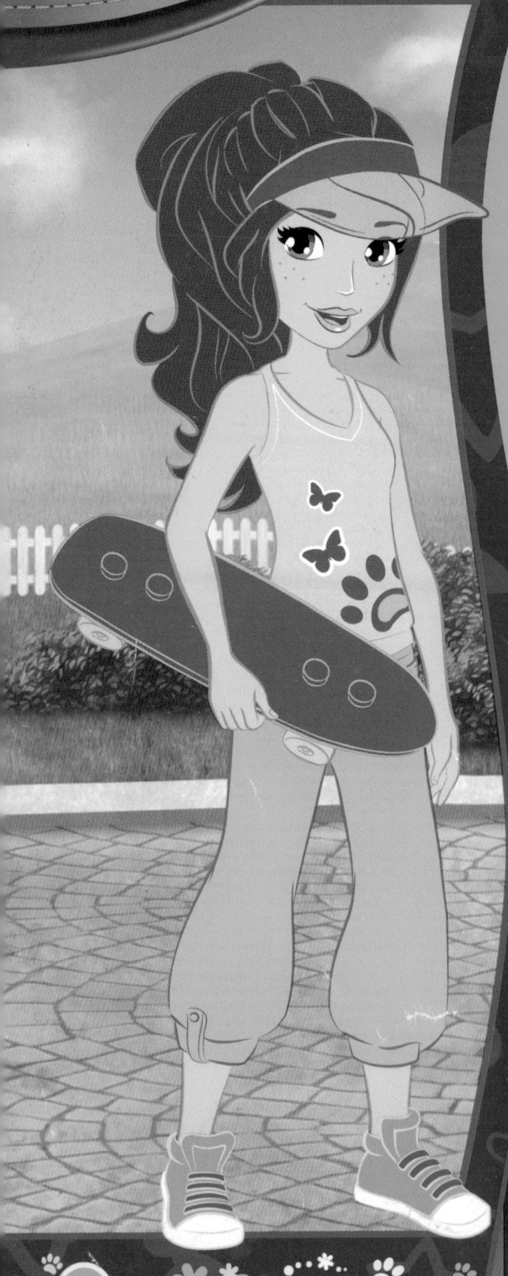

The animal lover of the group, Mia is a vegetarian. She enjoys taking care of and spending time with lots and lots of animals. She also excels at sports, drumming, and training animals. She spends her free time horse riding, camping, and doing magic tricks.

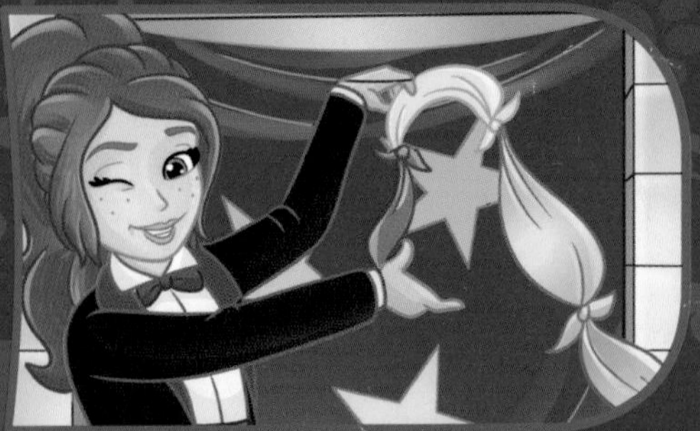

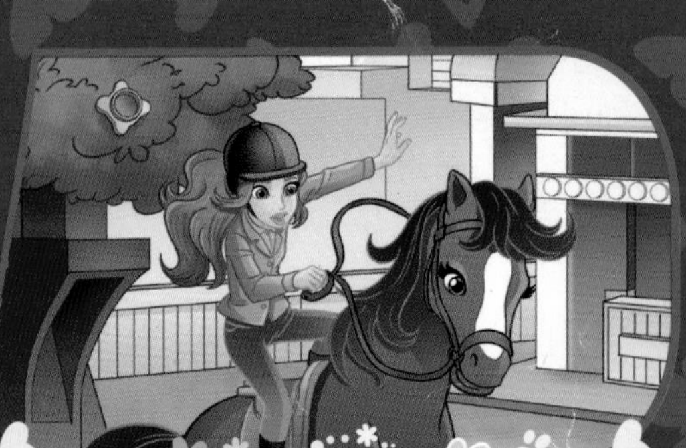

Olivia

Olivia loves science, nature, and history. If she could, she would spend all day inventing new things, as well as taking pictures and drawing. Super intelligent and focused, Olivia is quite a brain. She's still clumsy sometimes, but who isn't?

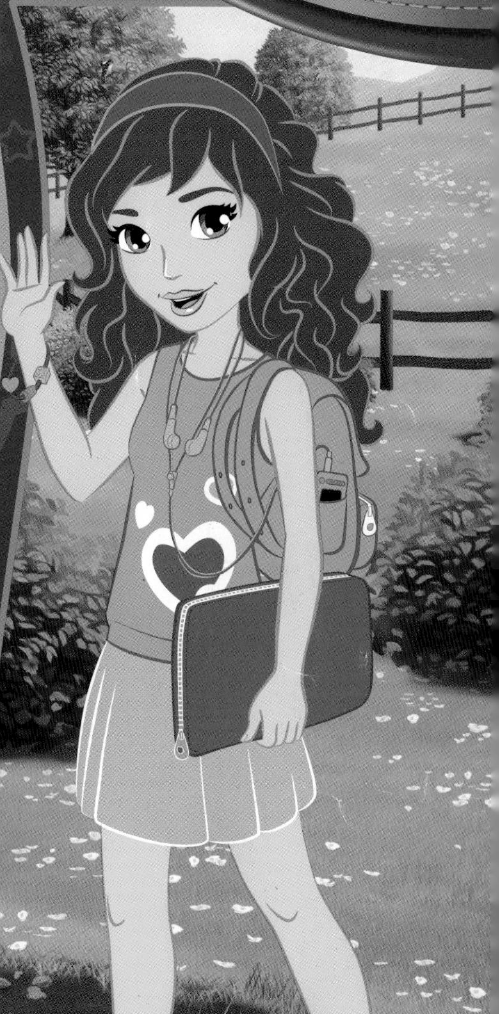

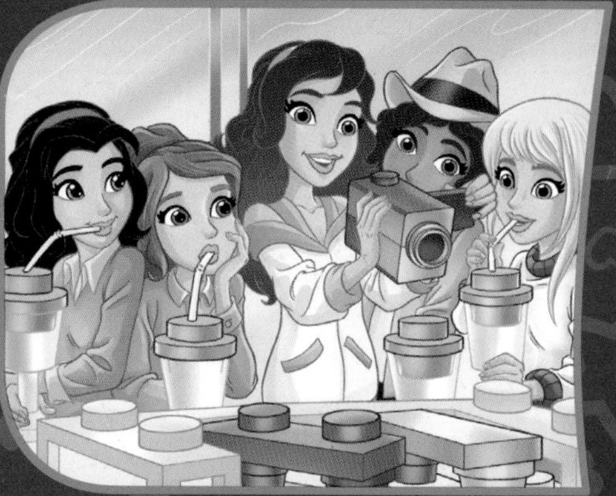

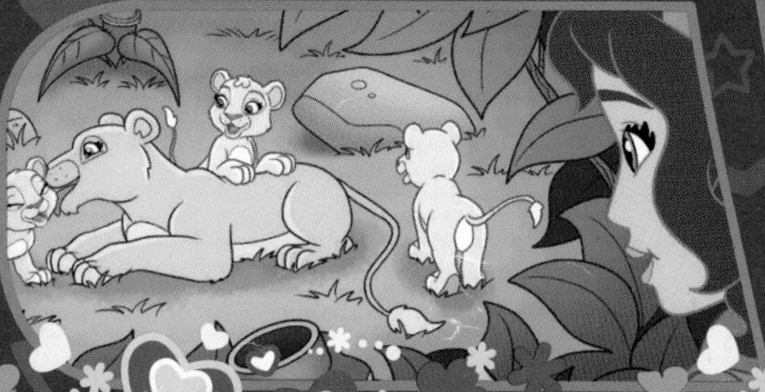

Stephanie

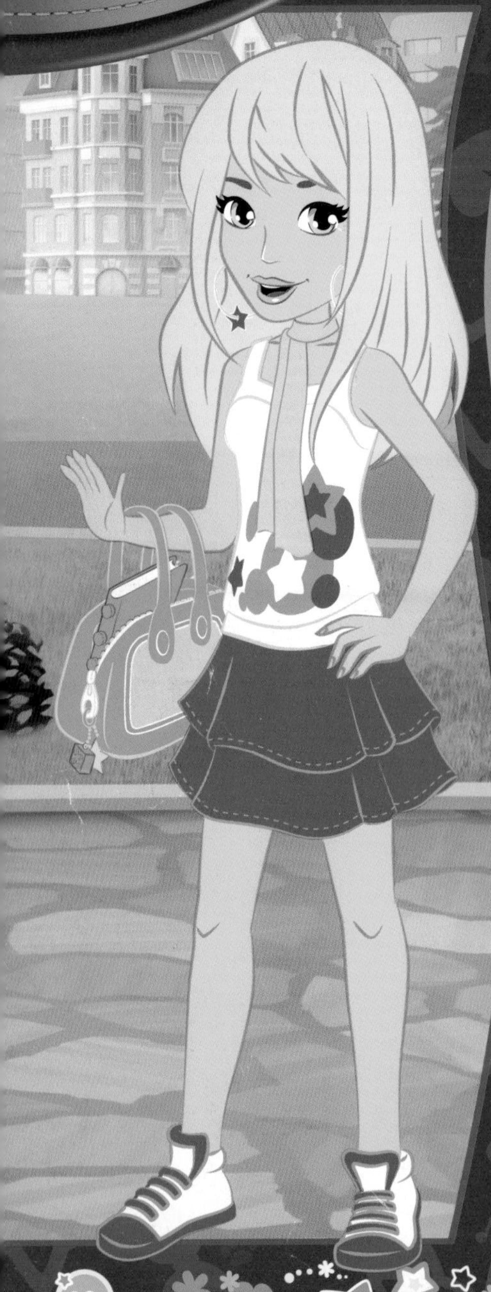

A confident natural leader, Stephanie is very social, creative, and organized. She loves planning events, parties, and soccer. She enjoys talking to people, writing stories, and dancing ballet. She is very down-to-earth, though at times a little bossy.

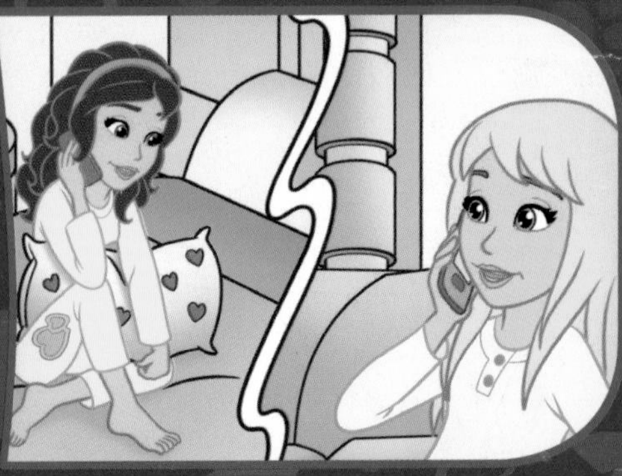

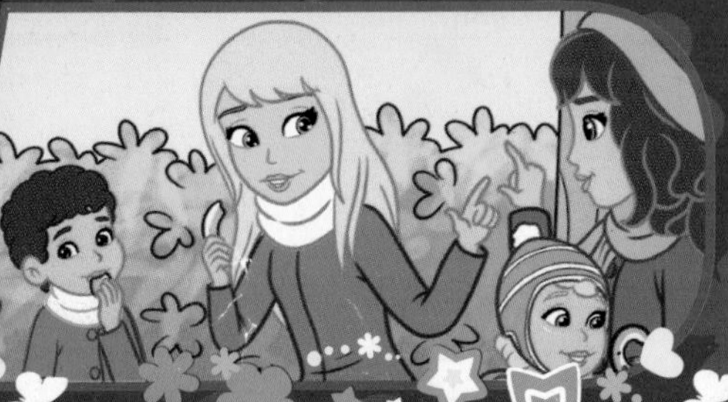

Friendship Tree in Danger

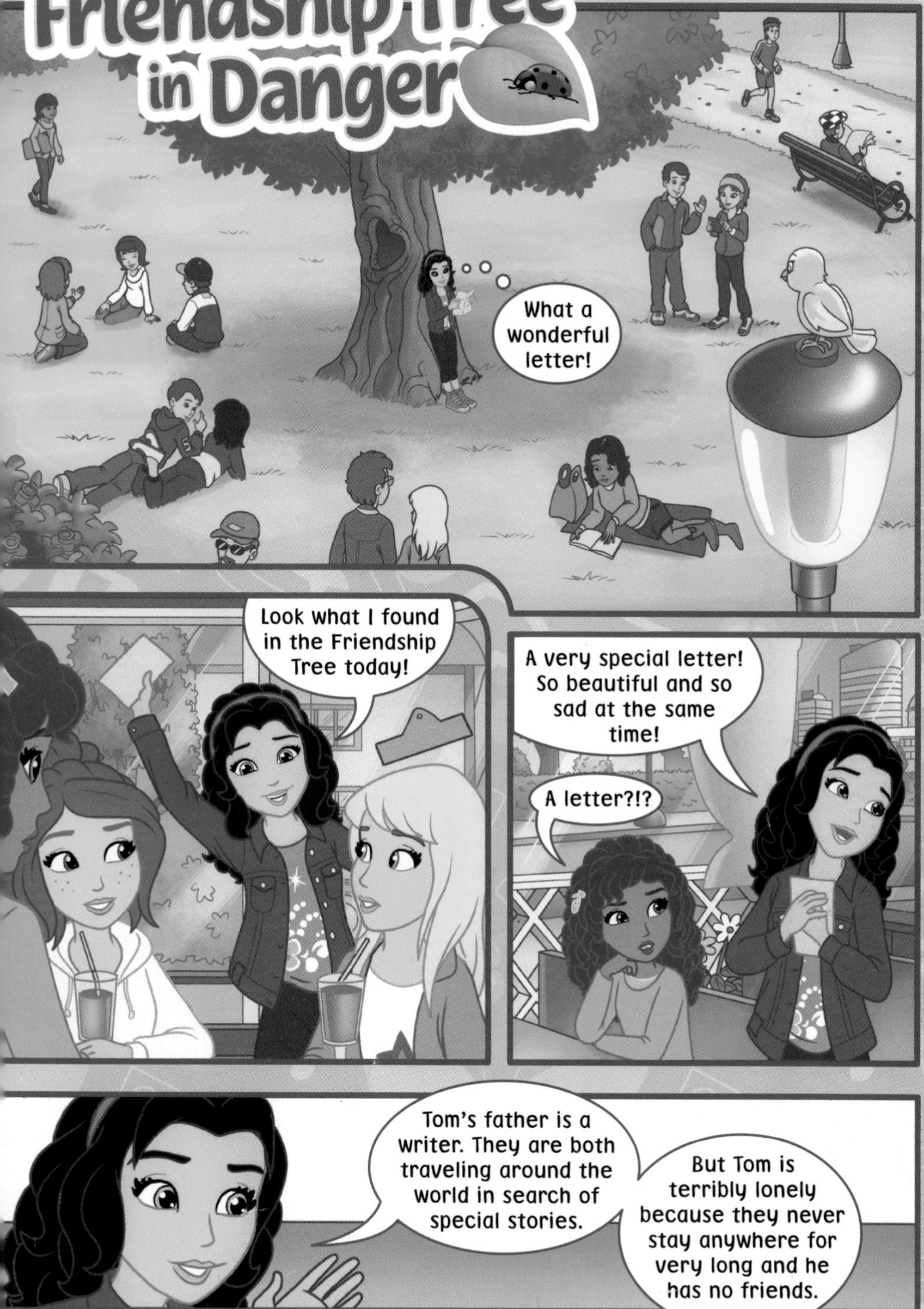
What a wonderful letter!
Look what I found in the Friendship Tree today!
A very special letter! So beautiful and so sad at the same time!
A letter?!?
Tom's father is a writer. They are both traveling around the world in search of special stories.
But Tom is terribly lonely because they never stay anywhere for very long and he has no friends.

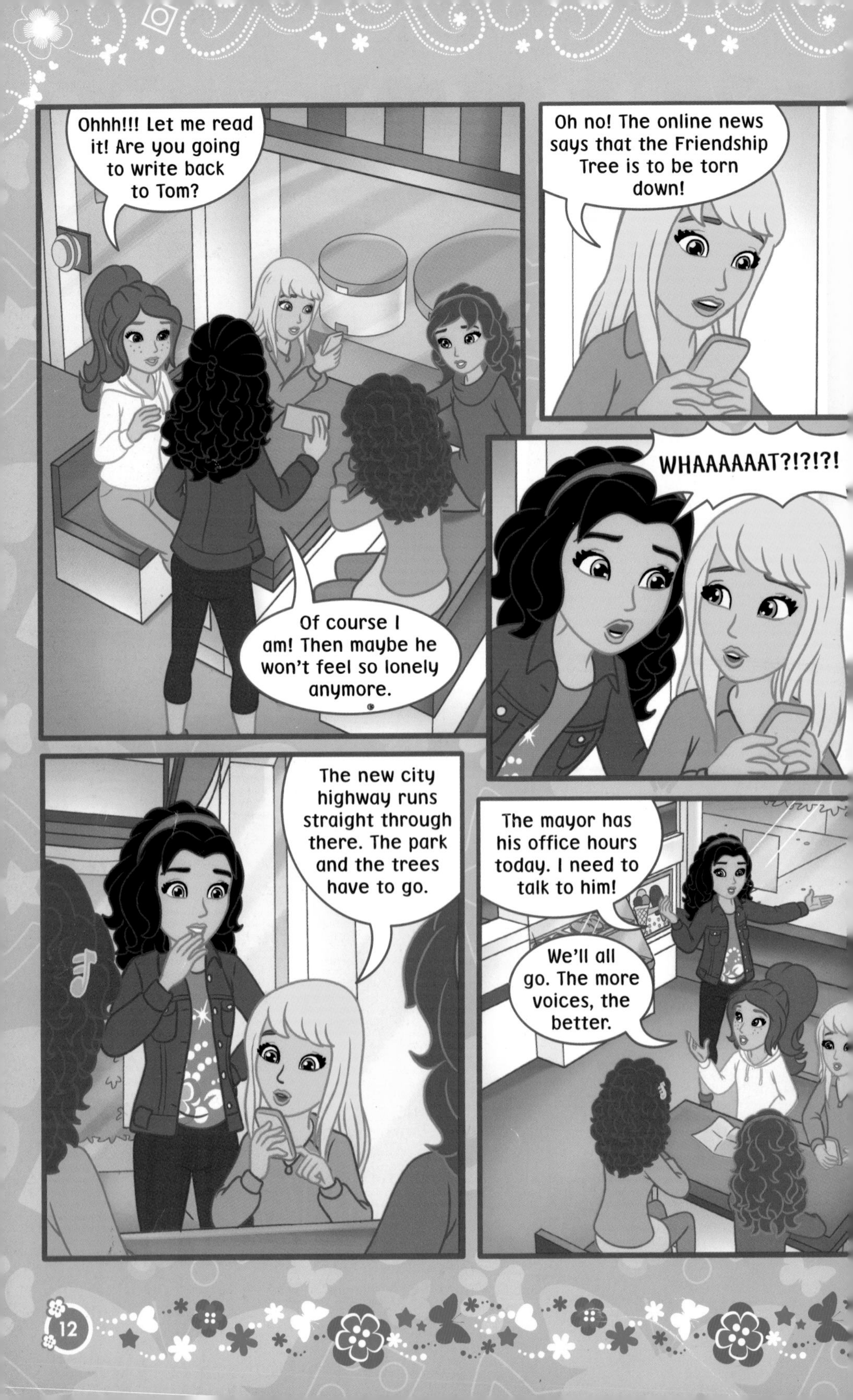
Ohhh!!! Let me read it! Are you going to write back to Tom?
Of course I am! Then maybe he won't feel so lonely anymore.
Oh no! The online news says that the Friendship Tree is to be torn down!
WHAAAAAAT?!?!?!
The new city highway runs straight through there. The park and the trees have to go.
The mayor has his office hours today. I need to talk to him!
We'll all go. The more voices, the better.

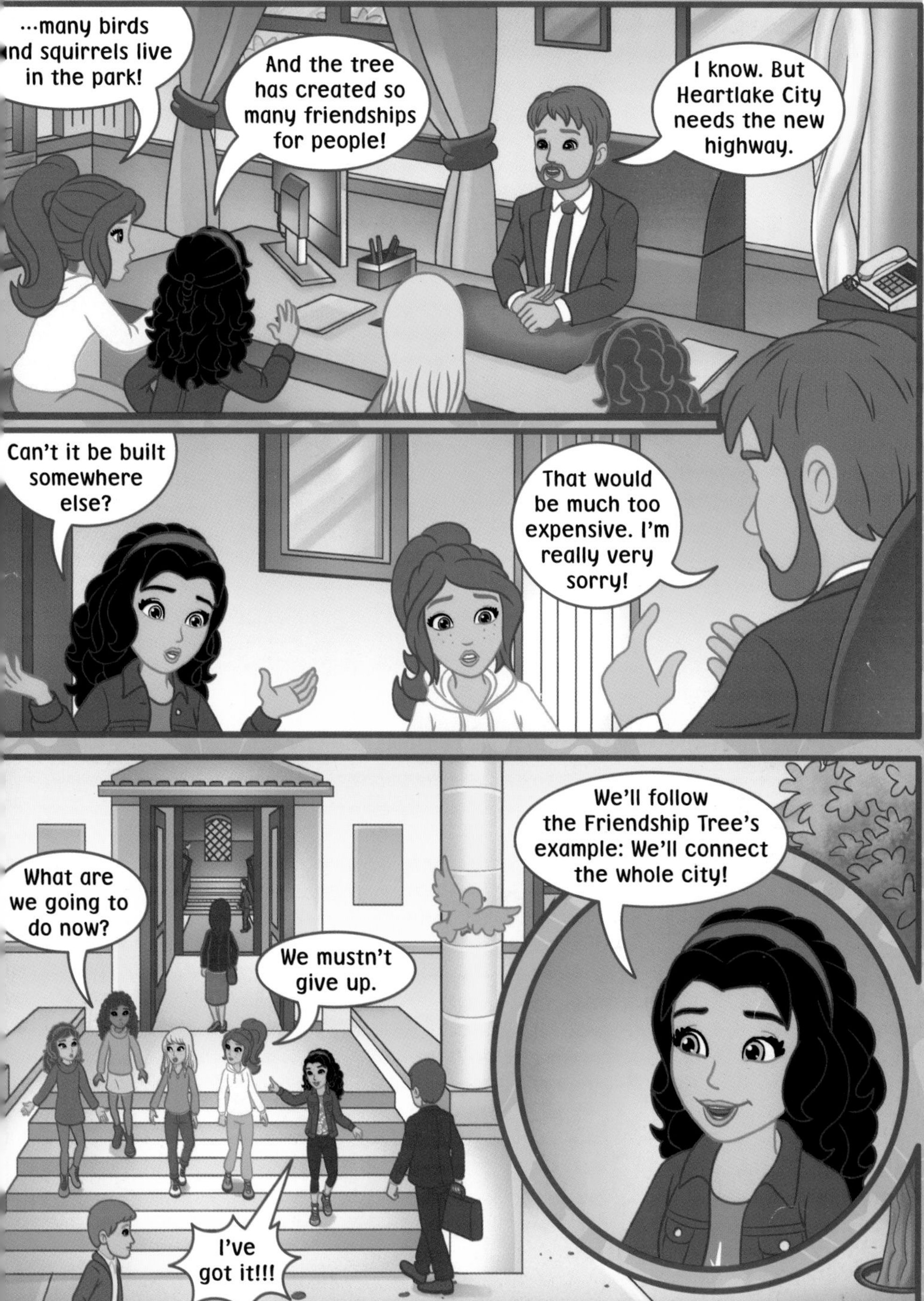
...many birds nd squirrels live in the park!
And the tree has created so many friendships for people!
I know. But Heartlake City needs the new highway.
Can't it be built somewhere else?
That would be much too expensive. I'm really very sorry!
What are we going to do now?
We mustn't give up.
I've got it!!!
We'll follow the Friendship Tree's example: We'll connect the whole city!

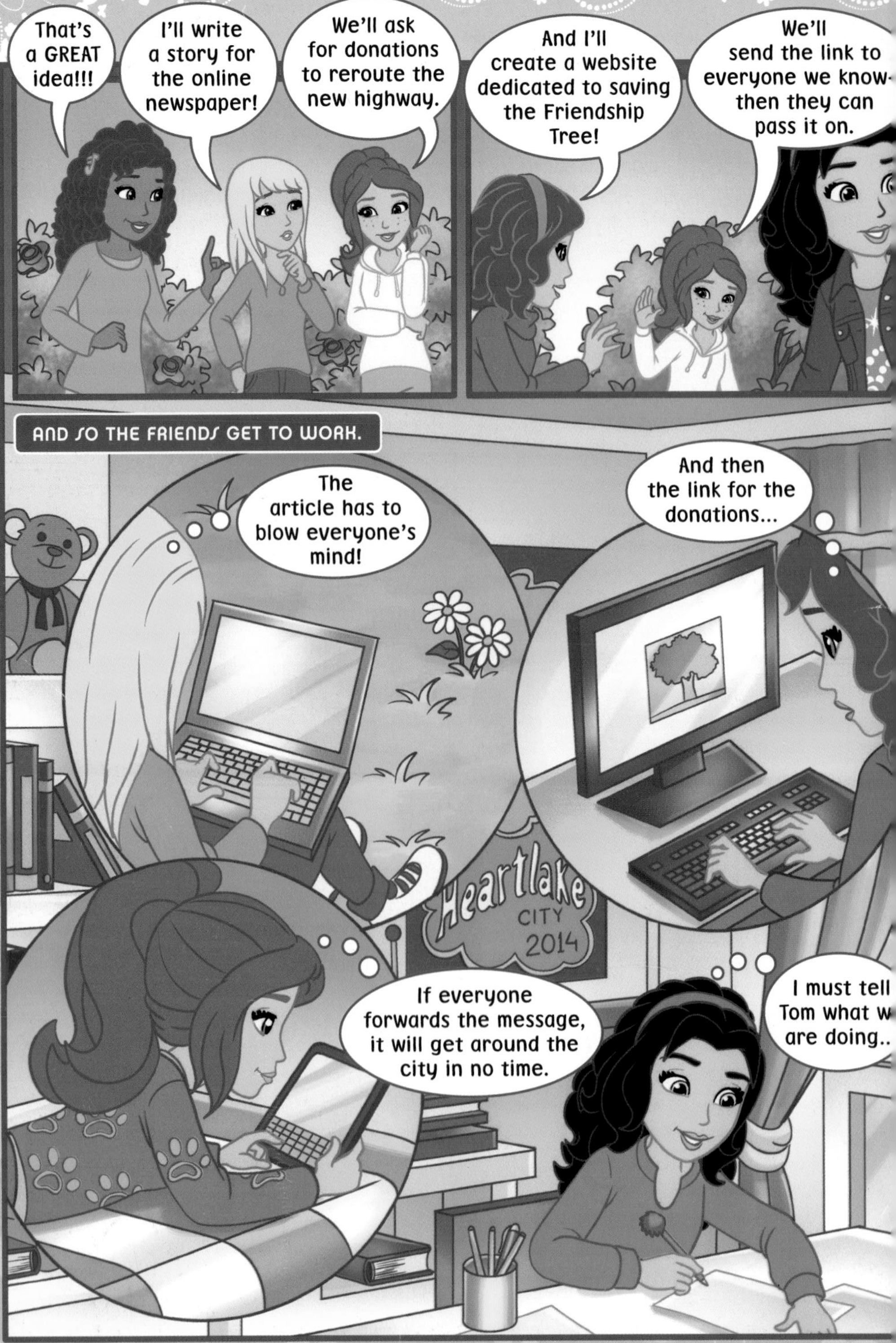
That's a GREAT idea!!!
I'll write a story for the online newspaper!
We'll ask for donations to reroute the new highway.
And I'll create a website dedicated to saving the Friendship Tree!
We'll send the link to everyone we know- then they can pass it on.
AND SO THE FRIENDS GET TO WORK.
The article has to blow everyone's mind!
And then the link for the donations...
Heartlake CITY 2014
If everyone forwards the message, it will get around the city in no time.
I must tell Tom what w are doing..

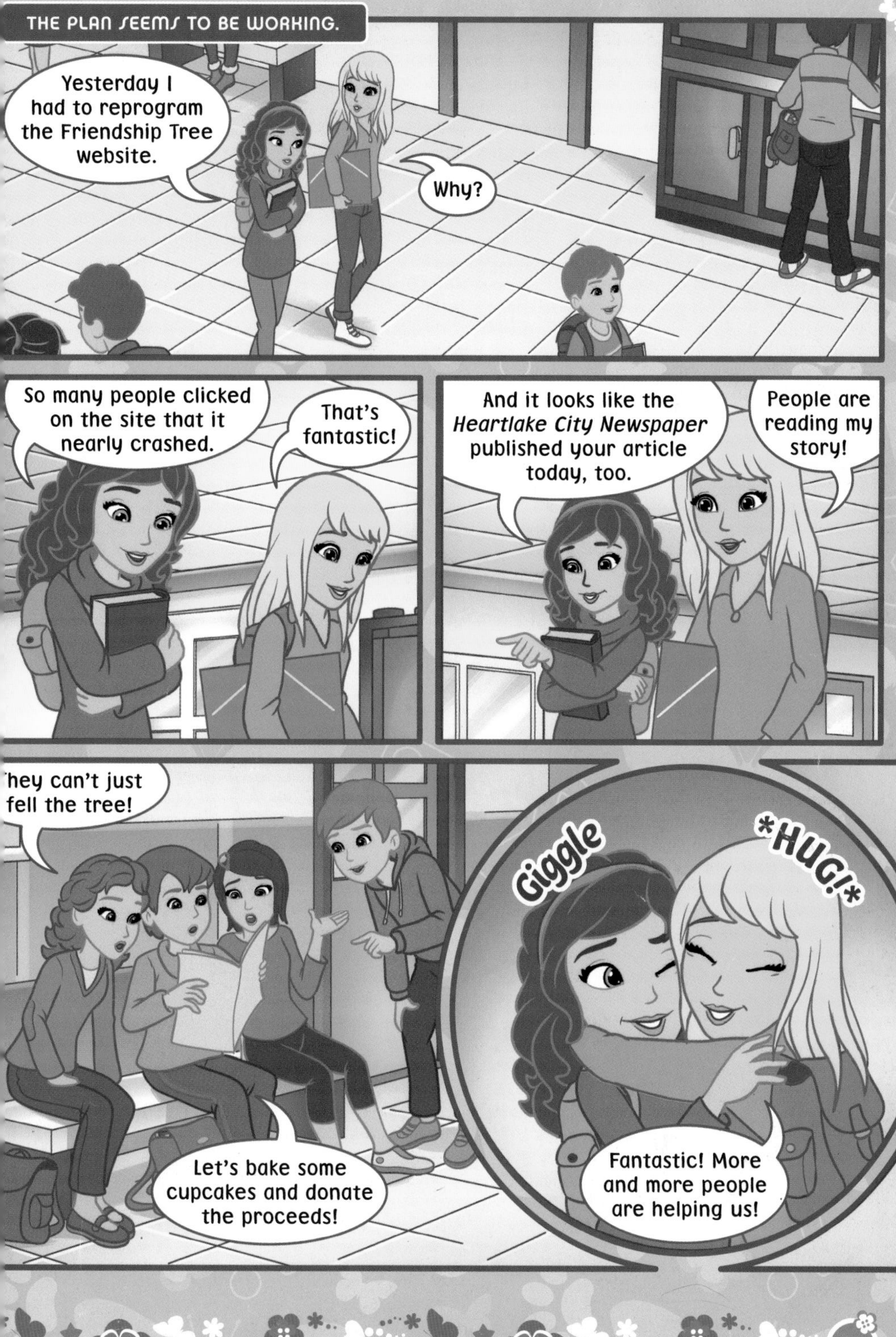
THE PLAN SEEMS TO BE WORKING.
Yesterday I had to reprogram the Friendship Tree website.
Why?
So many people clicked on the site that it nearly crashed.
That's fantastic!
And it looks like the *Heartlake City Newspaper* published your article today, too.
People are reading my story!
hey can't just fell the tree!
Let's bake some cupcakes and donate the proceeds!
Giggle
HUG!
Fantastic! More and more people are helping us!

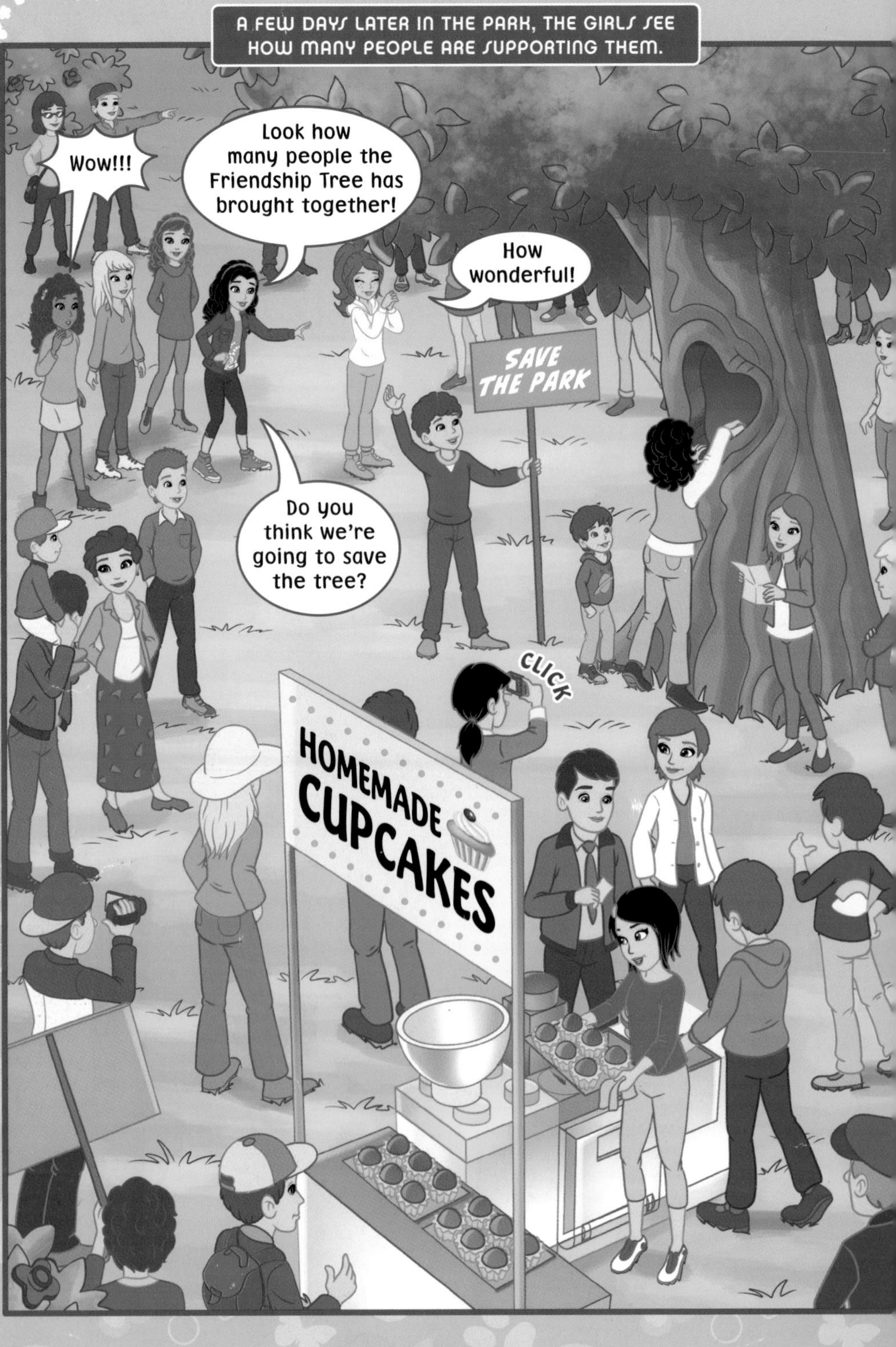
A FEW DAYS LATER IN THE PARK, THE GIRLS SEE HOW MANY PEOPLE ARE SUPPORTING THEM.
Wow!!!
Look how many people the Friendship Tree has brought together!
How wonderful!
SAVE THE PARK
Do you think we're going to save the tree?
CLICK
HOMEMADE CUPCAKES

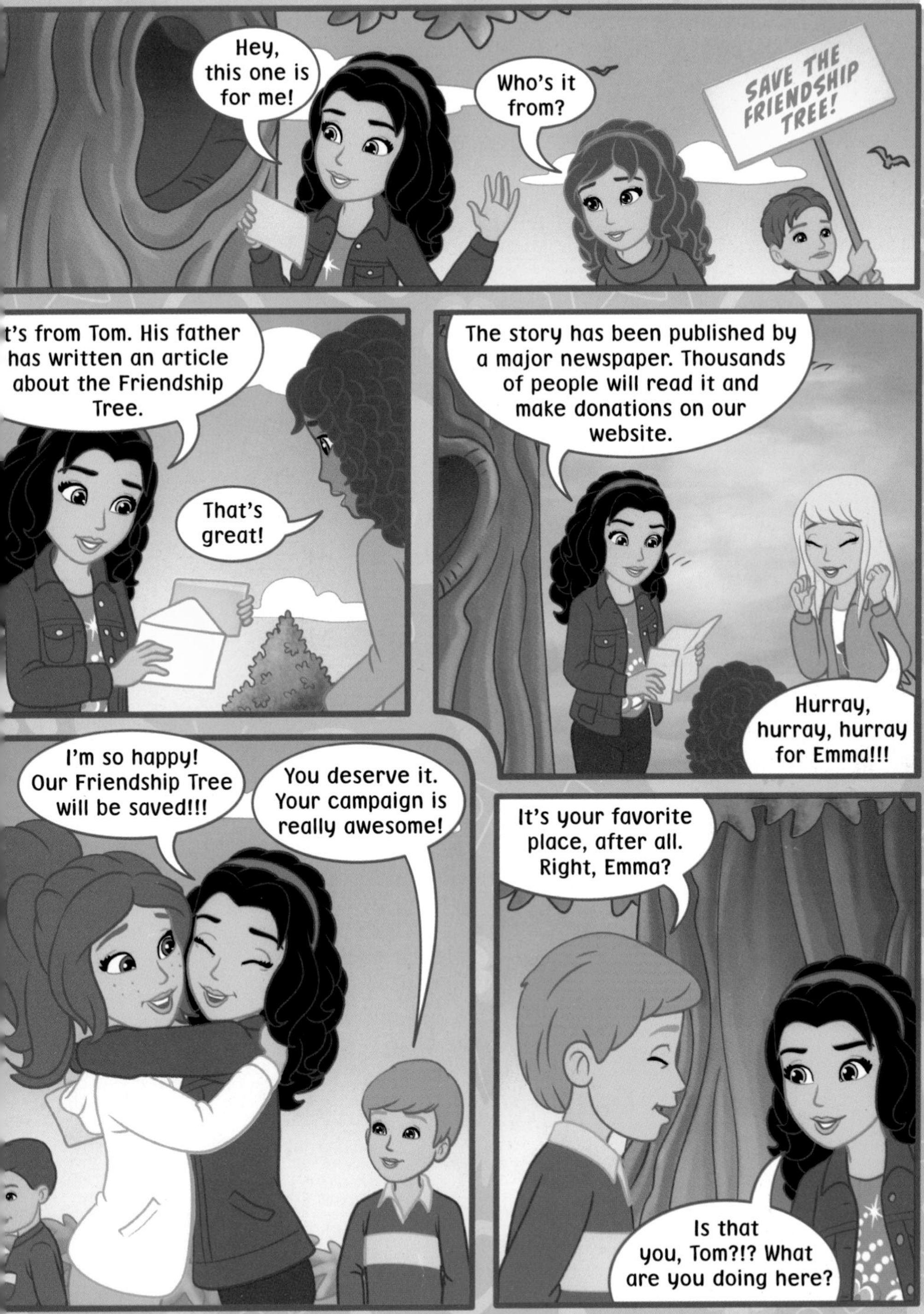
Hey, this one is for me!
Who's it from?
SAVE THE FRIENDSHIP TREE!
t's from Tom. His father has written an article about the Friendship Tree.
That's great!
The story has been published by a major newspaper. Thousands of people will read it and make donations on our website.
Hurray, hurray, hurray for Emma!!!
I'm so happy! Our Friendship Tree will be saved!!!
You deserve it. Your campaign is really awesome!
It's your favorite place, after all. Right, Emma?
Is that you, Tom?!? What are you doing here?

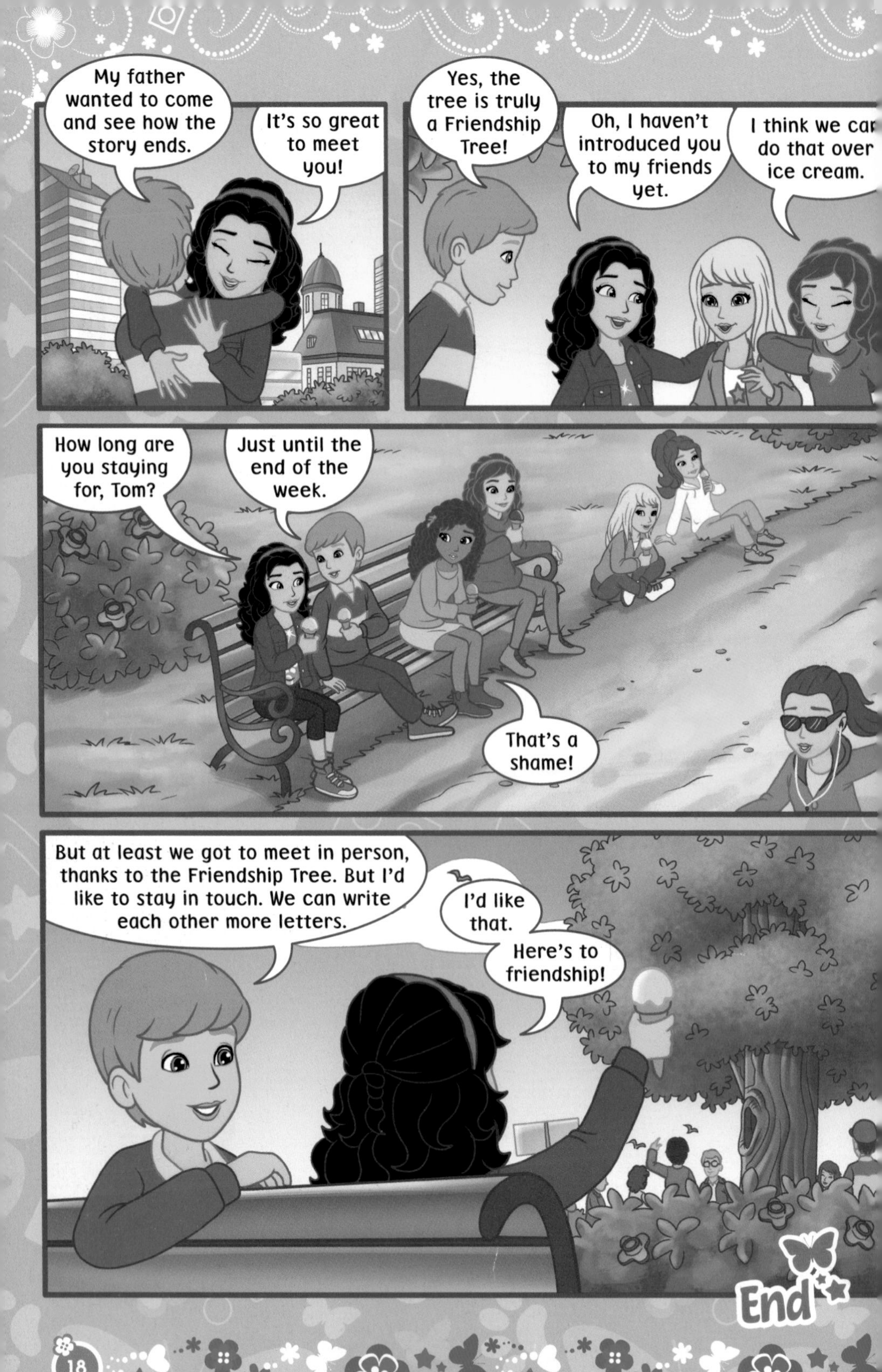
My father wanted to come and see how the story ends.
It's so great to meet you!
Yes, the tree is truly a Friendship Tree!
Oh, I haven't introduced you to my friends yet.
I think we ca do that over ice cream.
How long are you staying for, Tom?
Just until the end of the week.
That's a shame!
But at least we got to meet in person, thanks to the Friendship Tree. But I'd like to stay in touch. We can write each other more letters.
I'd like that.
Here's to friendship!
End

5 Awesome Ways to Help!

How Can YOU Make a Difference?

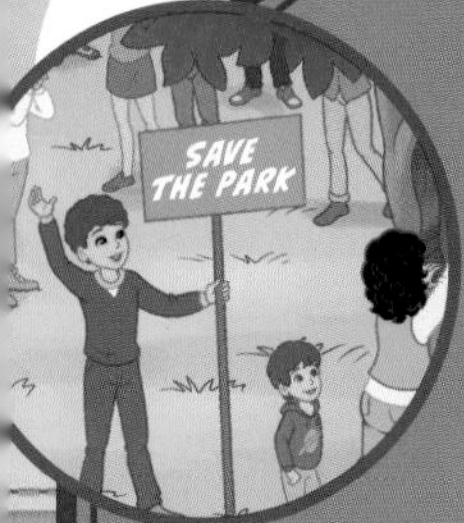
SAVE THE PARK

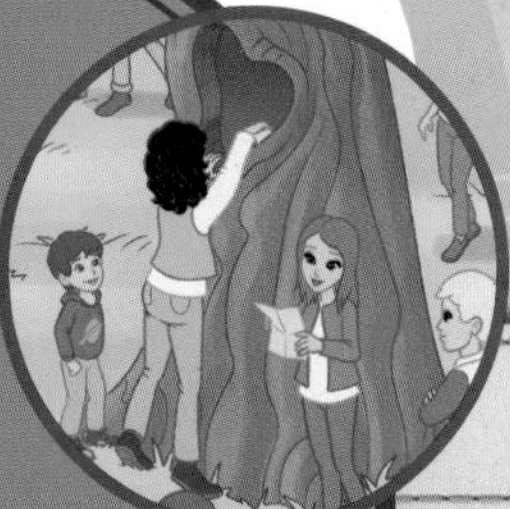

When Emma and her friends found out that the Friendship Tree was in danger of being cut down, they sprang into action to help save the tree. Have you ever wanted to do something to make a difference in your community but you didn't know how to get started? Now you do! Whether you want to start a recycling program, help raise money for charity, or donate things to people in need—no matter what the cause—there's always something you can do to help.

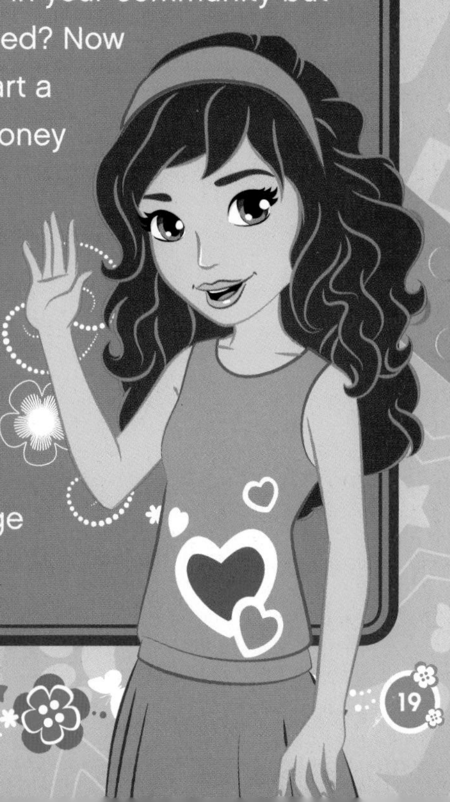

Check out this list of **5 Awesome Ways to Help** and get started making a change in your hometown!

1: Learn All About It

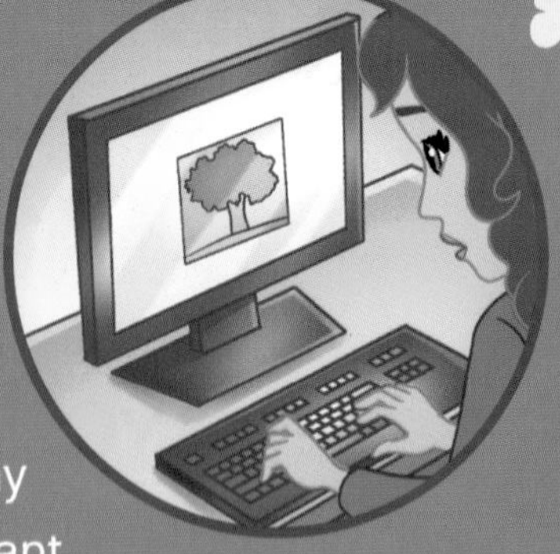

It's super important to educate yourself on whatever cause you're trying to help. The more you know, the more you can teach other people about why caring for this cause is so important. You can do research on the computer, ask your teacher to recommend some books on the subject, or go to the library and search for them yourself.

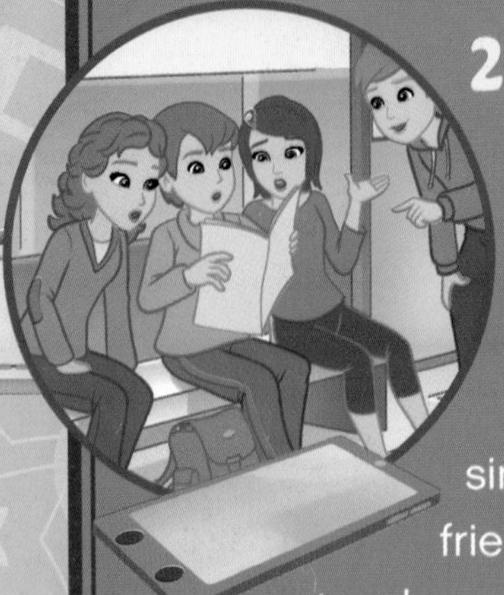

2: Spread the Word

Now that you know a lot about the cause you are trying to help, spread the word to other people and explain why this cause needs their help, too. You can do this by simply starting a conversation with a friend about the subject, talking to your teacher about including it in one of your school lessons, or even filming a video of yourself talking about the cause and showing it to friends and family.

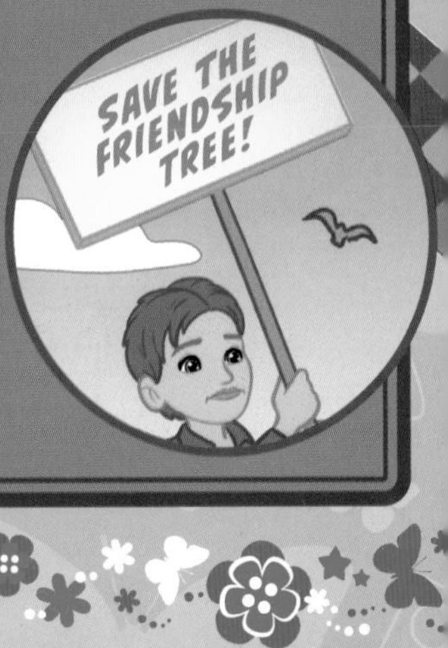
SAVE THE FRIENDSHIP TREE!

3: Volunteer

There are already many ways to volunteer in your community, so ask your parents or a teacher to help you find the type of volunteer activity that is right for you. Giving your time is so rewarding, and every little bit counts.

4: Throw a Fundraiser

Just like the LEGO Friends who helped save their tree, you can have your own fundraiser to help raise money for your cause. It can be as small as having a bake sale or a lemonade stand on your front lawn and donating the money you make, or talking to your teacher or principal about organizing something larger in your school.

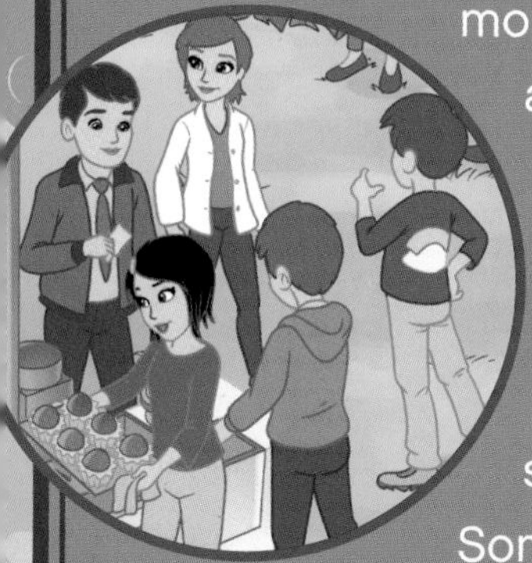

Some great ideas for fundraisers include talent shows, carnivals, fashion shows, or sports events. You can sell tickets and food, and raffle off prizes—all for a cause!

5: Write a Letter

Writing a letter to a local government official, newspaper editor, or city council member is an important way to make a difference. You're not the only one who thinks your cause is important. If everyone who thinks your cause is important writes a letter, that's a lot of letters! Together, they can all make a difference.

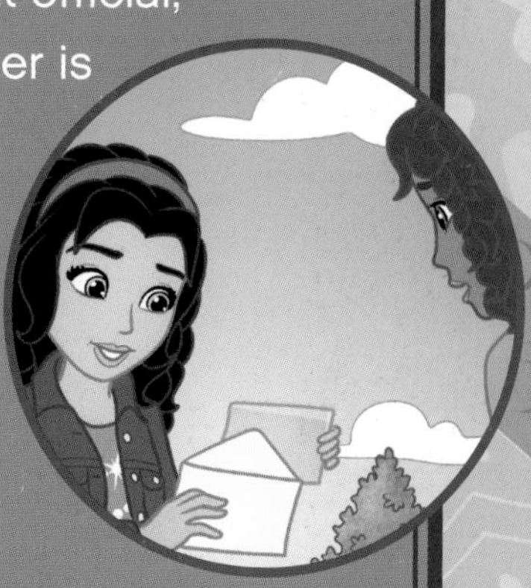

Lion in Distress

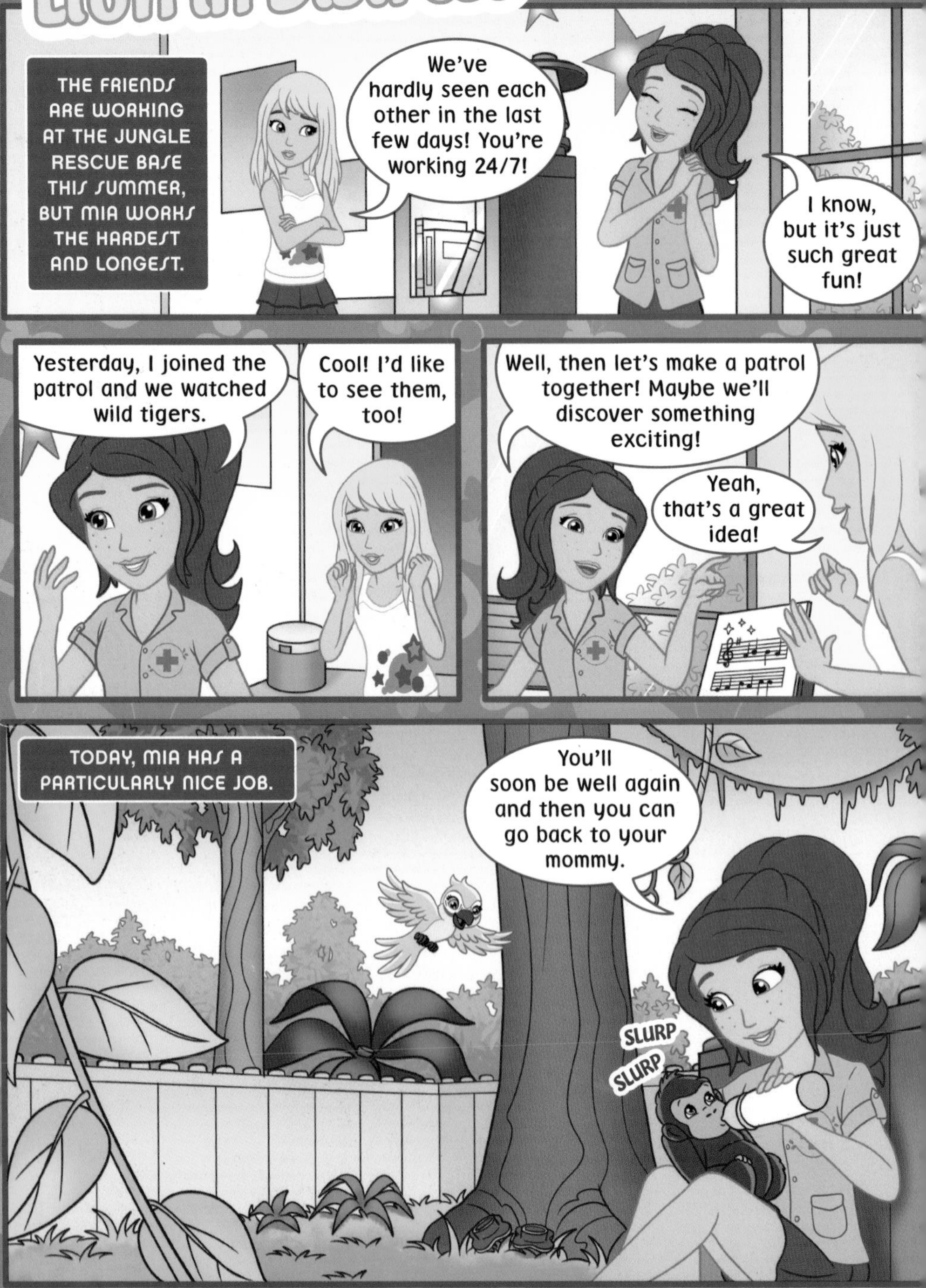
THE FRIENDS ARE WORKING AT THE JUNGLE RESCUE BASE THIS SUMMER, BUT MIA WORKS THE HARDEST AND LONGEST.
We've hardly seen each other in the last few days! You're working 24/7!
I know, but it's just such great fun!
Yesterday, I joined the patrol and we watched wild tigers.
Cool! I'd like to see them, too!
Well, then let's make a patrol together! Maybe we'll discover something exciting!
Yeah, that's a great idea!
TODAY, MIA HAS A PARTICULARLY NICE JOB.
You'll soon be well again and then you can go back to your mommy.
SLURP
SLURP

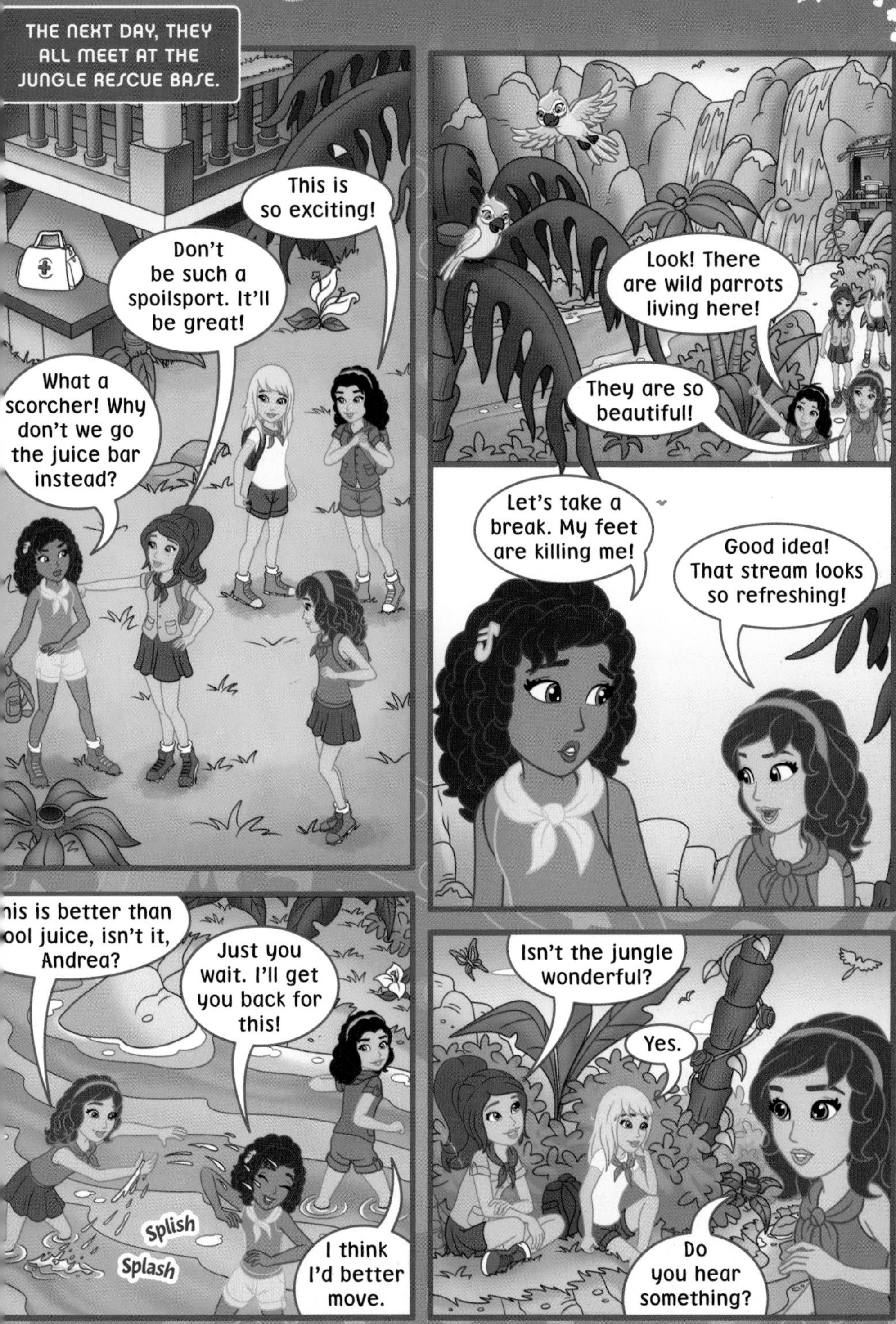
THE NEXT DAY, THEY ALL MEET AT THE JUNGLE RESCUE BASE.
This is so exciting!
Don't be such a spoilsport. It'll be great!
What a scorcher! Why don't we go the juice bar instead?
Look! There are wild parrots living here!
They are so beautiful!
Let's take a break. My feet are killing me!
Good idea! That stream looks so refreshing!
his is better than ool juice, isn't it, Andrea?
Just you wait. I'll get you back for this!
Splish
Splash
I think I'd better move.
Isn't the jungle wonderful?
Yes.
Do you hear something?

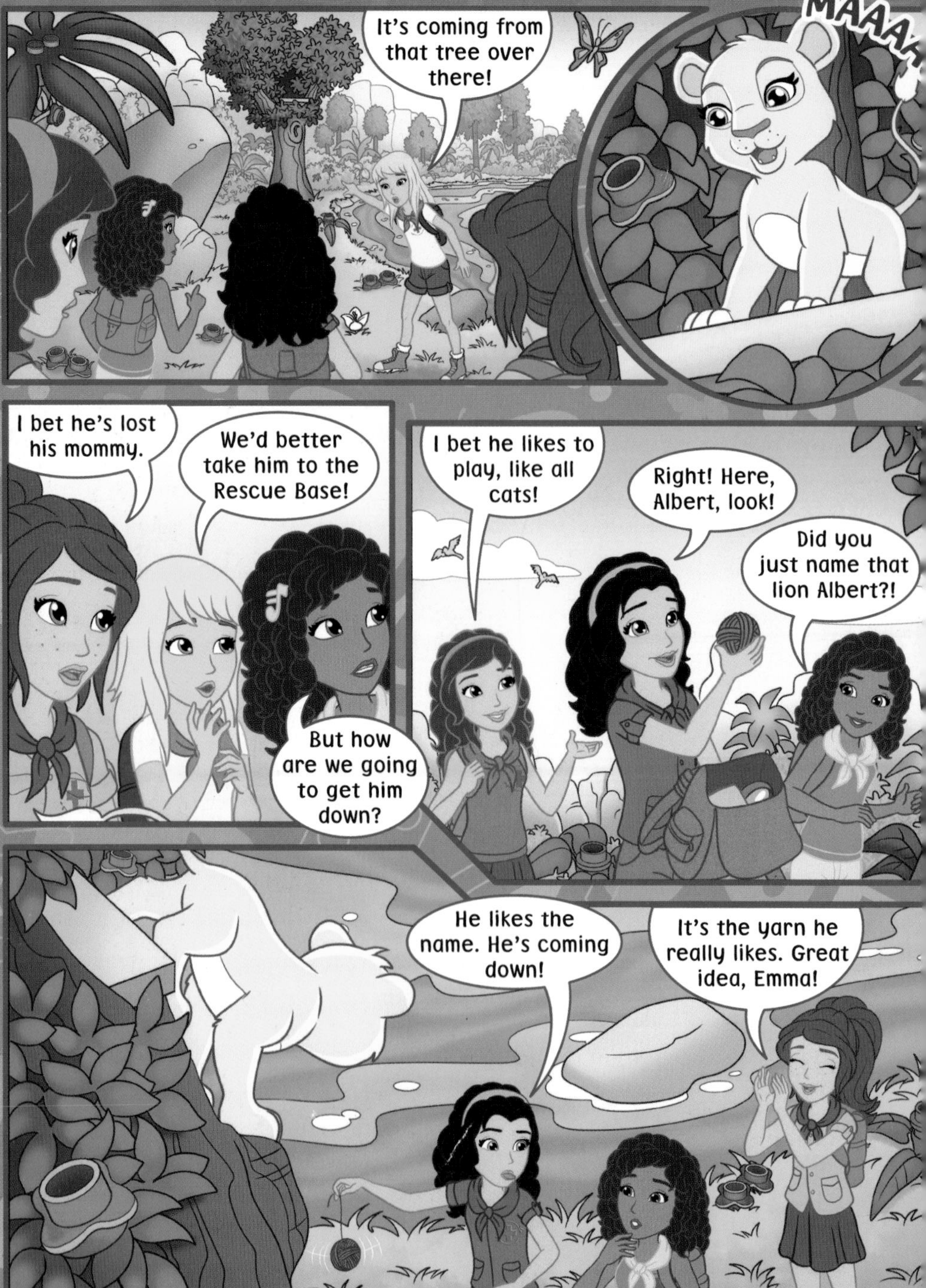
It's coming from that tree over there!
MAAA
I bet he's lost his mommy.
We'd better take him to the Rescue Base!
But how are we going to get him down?
I bet he likes to play, like all cats!
Right! Here, Albert, look!
Did you just name that lion Albert?!
He likes the name. He's coming down!
It's the yarn he really likes. Great idea, Emma!

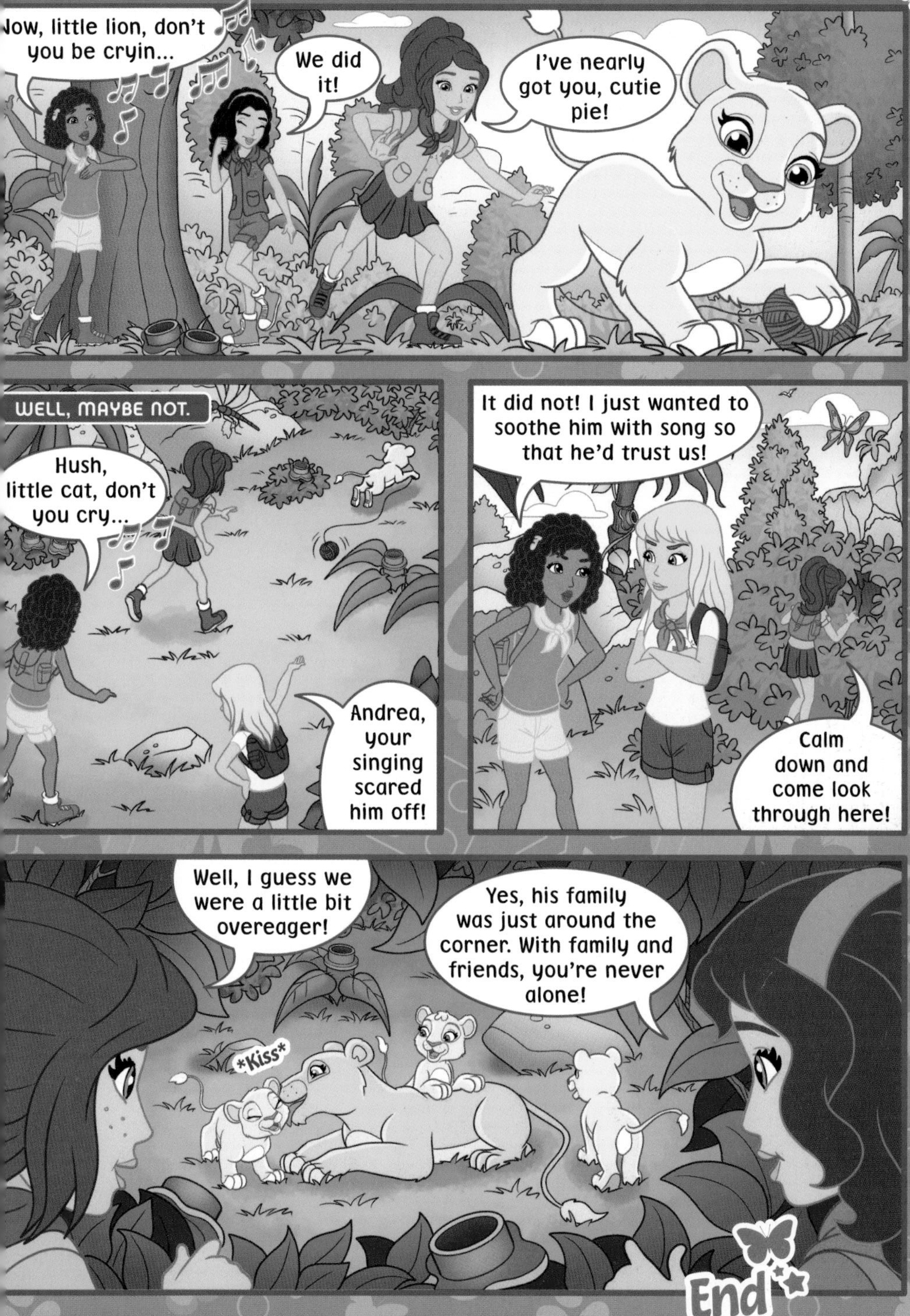
Now, little lion, don't you be cryin...
We did it!
I've nearly got you, cutie pie!
WELL, MAYBE NOT.
Hush, little cat, don't you cry...
Andrea, your singing scared him off!
It did not! I just wanted to soothe him with song so that he'd trust us!
Calm down and come look through here!
Well, I guess we were a little bit overeager!
Yes, his family was just around the corner. With family and friends, you're never alone!
Kiss
End

More About Lions

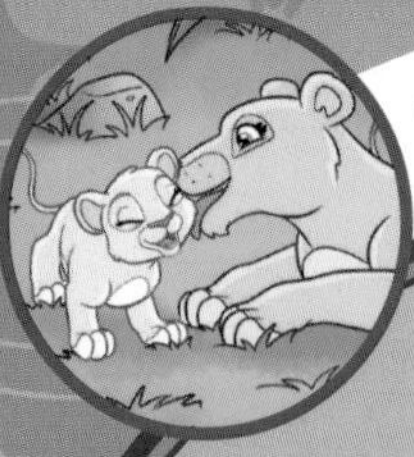

The King of the Jungle

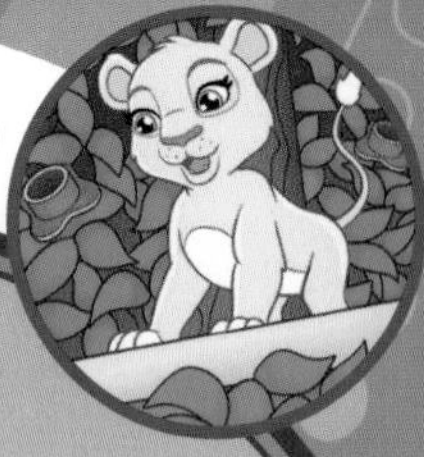

The lion is known as the king of the jungle for its courage and beauty, even though it doesn't actually live in the jungle. Lions live in southern Africa—in the Sahara—in eastern Africa, and some parts of India. Did you know that lions are the only kind of cats that live in groups? A group of lions is called a "pride." A pride is made up of a family of lions. These prides, which can be as large as fifteen or twenty lions, are made up mostly of female lions and their young, and usually have between one and three male lions leading the

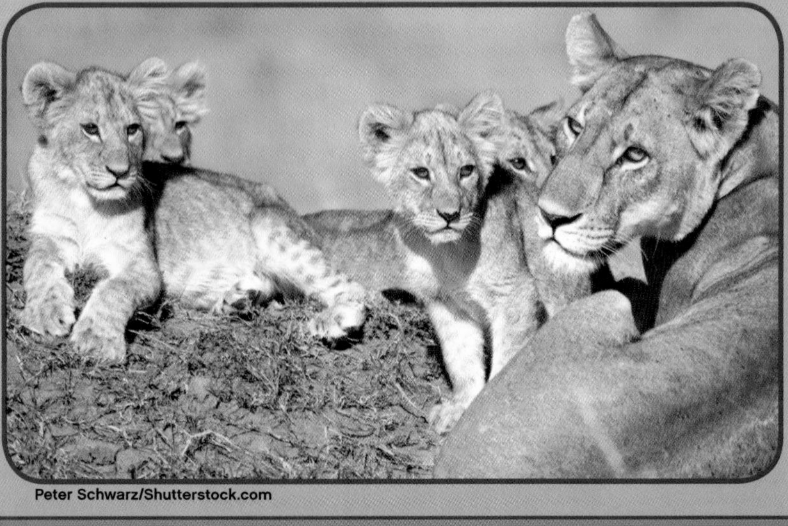

Peter Schwarz/Shutterstock.com

group. Female lions are the pride's hunters (cool, huh?), while the male lions protect and defend the pride from attackers. When a female lion gives birth to her cubs, she hides them from the pride for up to six weeks to protect them from the other members of the pride. You're probably wondering why she does this, aren't you? She hides her cubs because grown lions will harm cubs that they don't recognize immediately as family. The mother will only visit her cubs to feed them. It's lucky that cubs are born with spotted coats so they can blend in with their habitats! (Actually, it's not *exactly* luck; it's the way nature works.) When the mother is ready to introduce them to the pride, she must do so carefully—very carefully!

Stuart G Porter/Shutterstock.com

Fab Facts:

- ✿ A lion's roar can be heard from five miles away!
- ✿ Male lions can be up to eight feet long and can weigh up to five hundred pounds.
- ✿ Lion cubs are born blind.
- ✿ The lion's mane only grows on male lions and can be used to scare away attackers or to attract female lions.

It's Child's Play! (... or Not?)

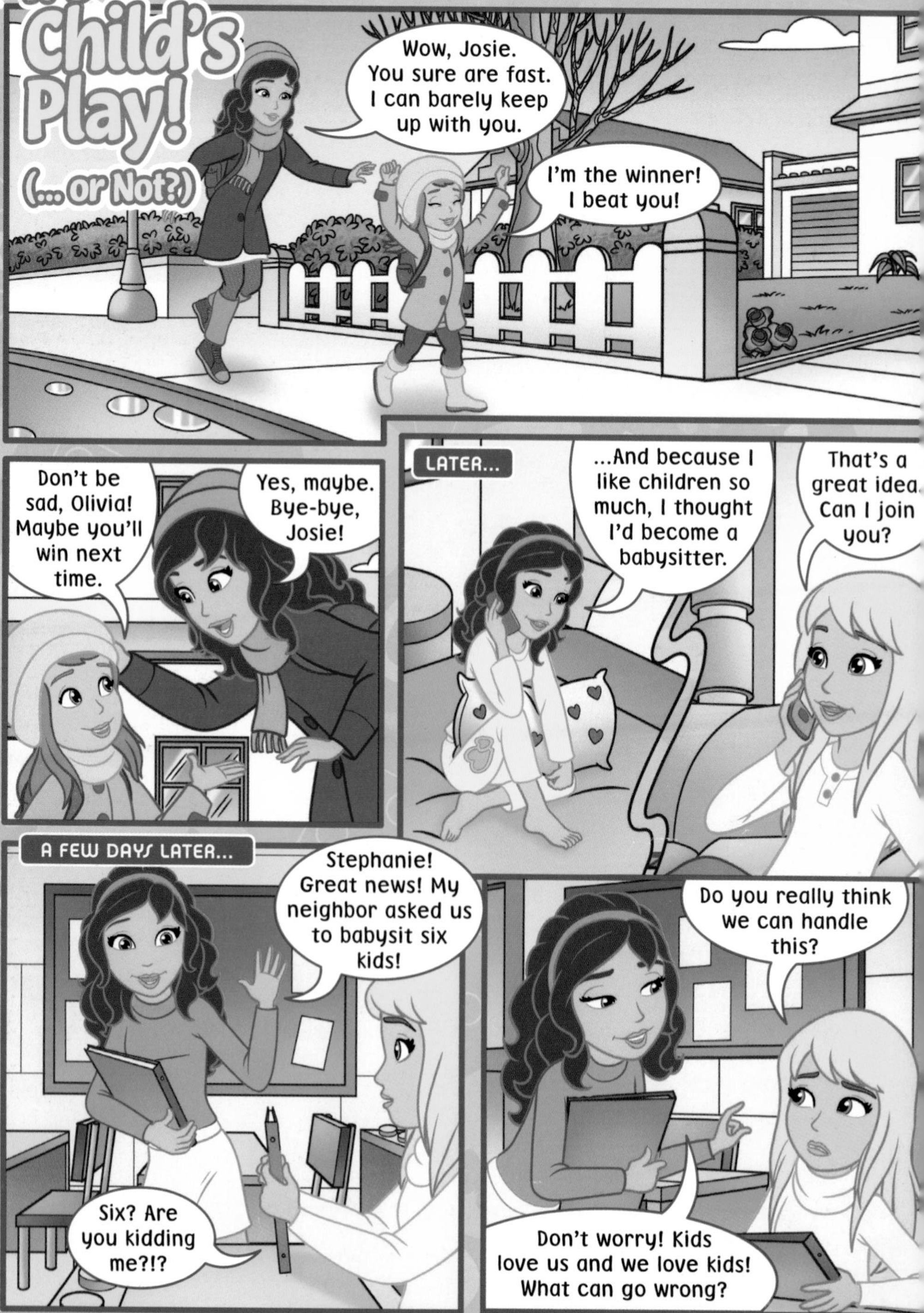

Wow, Josie. You sure are fast. I can barely keep up with you.
I'm the winner! I beat you!
Don't be sad, Olivia! Maybe you'll win next time.
Yes, maybe. Bye-bye, Josie!
LATER...
...And because I like children so much, I thought I'd become a babysitter.
That's a great idea. Can I join you?
A FEW DAYS LATER...
Stephanie! Great news! My neighbor asked us to babysit six kids!
Six? Are you kidding me?!?
Do you really think we can handle this?
Don't worry! Kids love us and we love kids! What can go wrong?

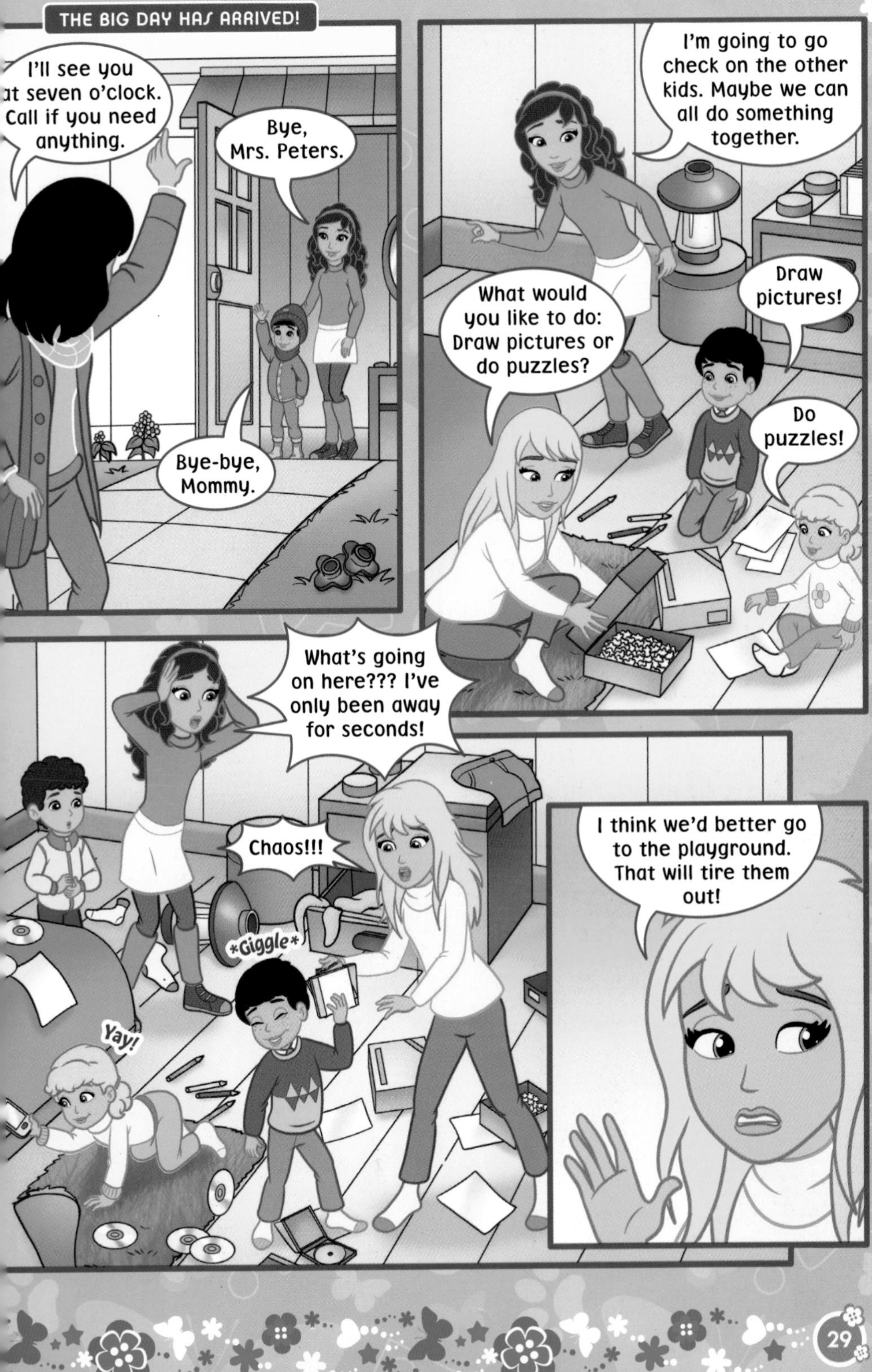
THE BIG DAY HAS ARRIVED!
I'll see you at seven o'clock. Call if you need anything.
Bye, Mrs. Peters.
Bye-bye, Mommy.
I'm going to go check on the other kids. Maybe we can all do something together.
What would you like to do: Draw pictures or do puzzles?
Draw pictures!
Do puzzles!
What's going on here??? I've only been away for seconds!
Chaos!!!
Giggle
Yay!
I think we'd better go to the playground. That will tire them out!

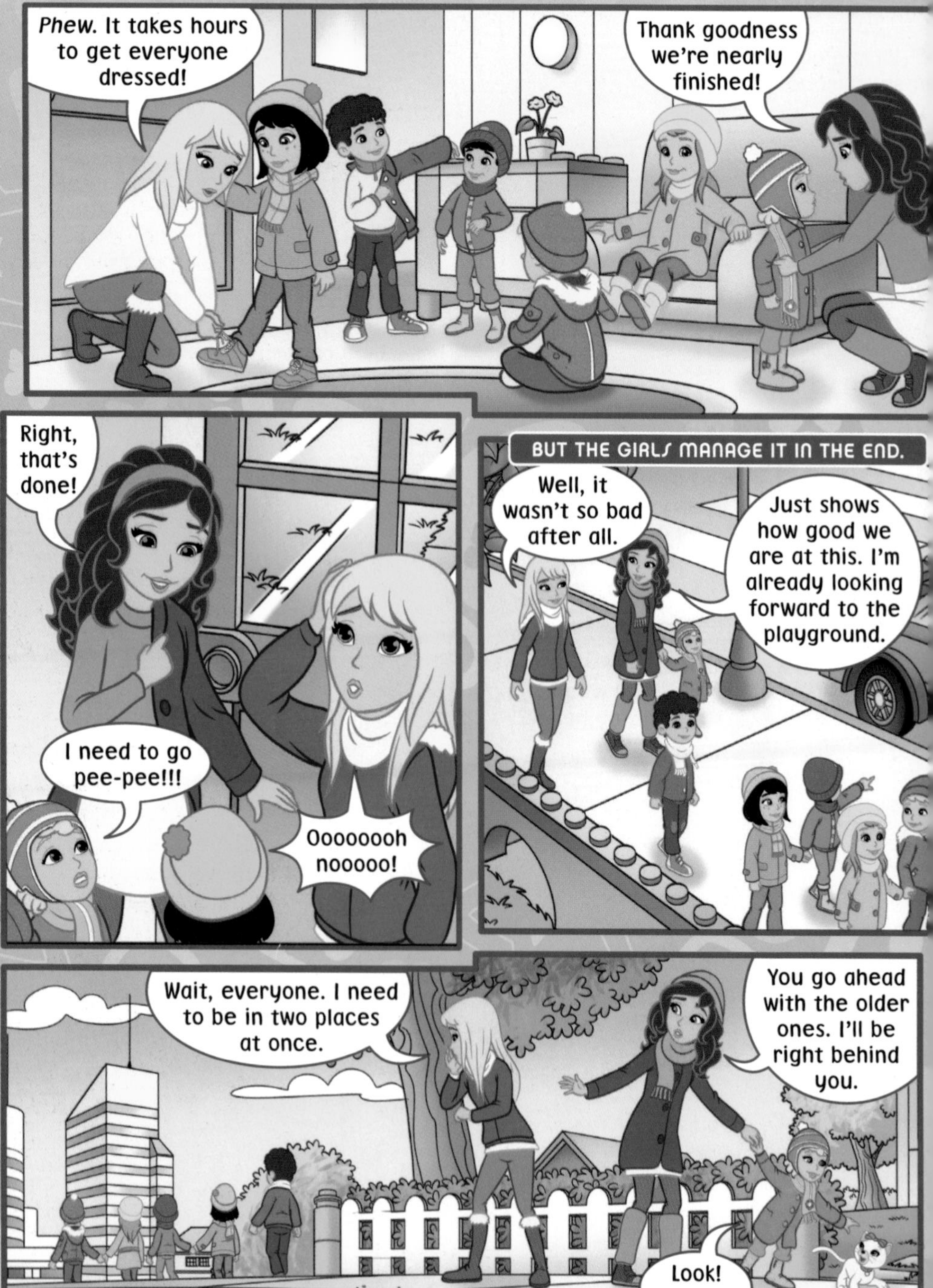
Phew. It takes hours to get everyone dressed!
Thank goodness we're nearly finished!
Right, that's done!
I need to go pee-pee!!!
Oooooooh nooooo!
BUT THE GIRLS MANAGE IT IN THE END.
Well, it wasn't so bad after all.
Just shows how good we are at this. I'm already looking forward to the playground.
Wait, everyone. I need to be in two places at once.
You go ahead with the older ones. I'll be right behind you.
Look! A kitty!

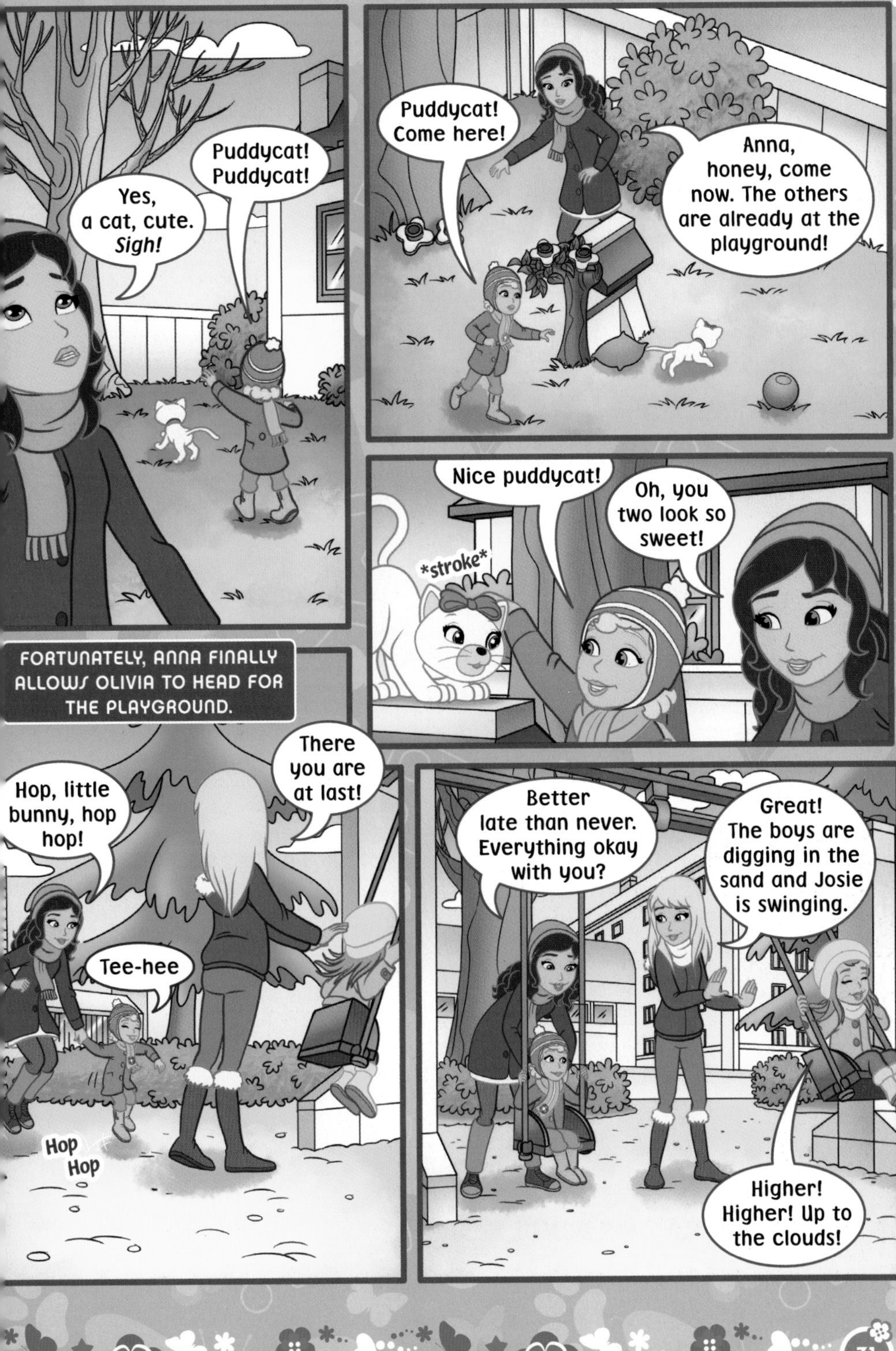

Puddycat! Puddycat!
Yes, a cat, cute. *Sigh!*
Puddycat! Come here!
Anna, honey, come now. The others are already at the playground!
Nice puddycat!
stroke
Oh, you two look so sweet!
FORTUNATELY, ANNA FINALLY ALLOWS OLIVIA TO HEAD FOR THE PLAYGROUND.
Hop, little bunny, hop hop!
There you are at last!
Tee-hee
Hop Hop
Better late than never. Everything okay with you?
Great! The boys are digging in the sand and Josie is swinging.
Higher! Higher! Up to the clouds!

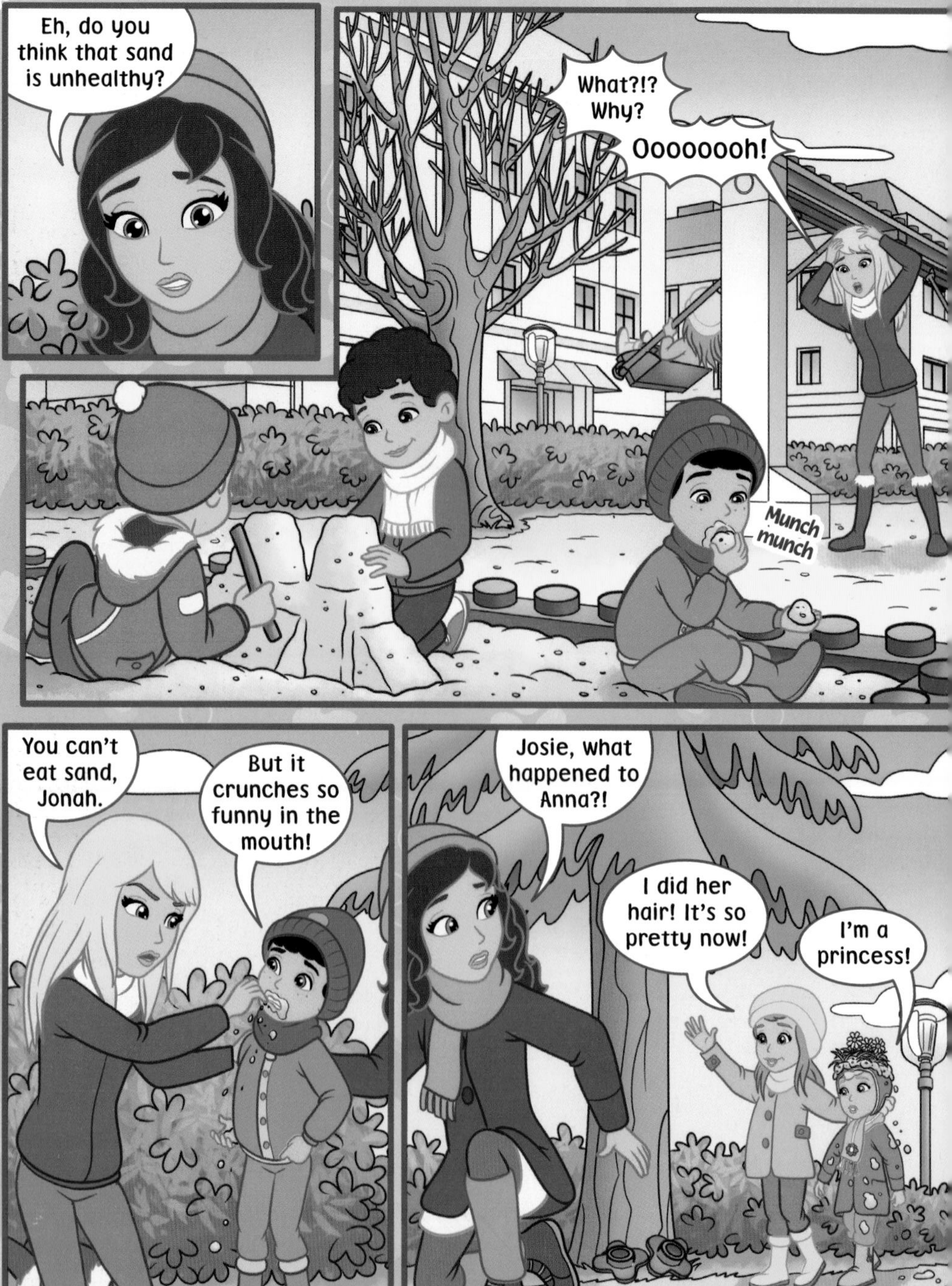
Eh, do you think that sand is unhealthy?
What?!? Why?
Oooooooh!
Munch munch
You can't eat sand, Jonah.
But it crunches so funny in the mouth!
Josie, what happened to Anna?!
I did her hair! It's so pretty now!
I'm a princess!

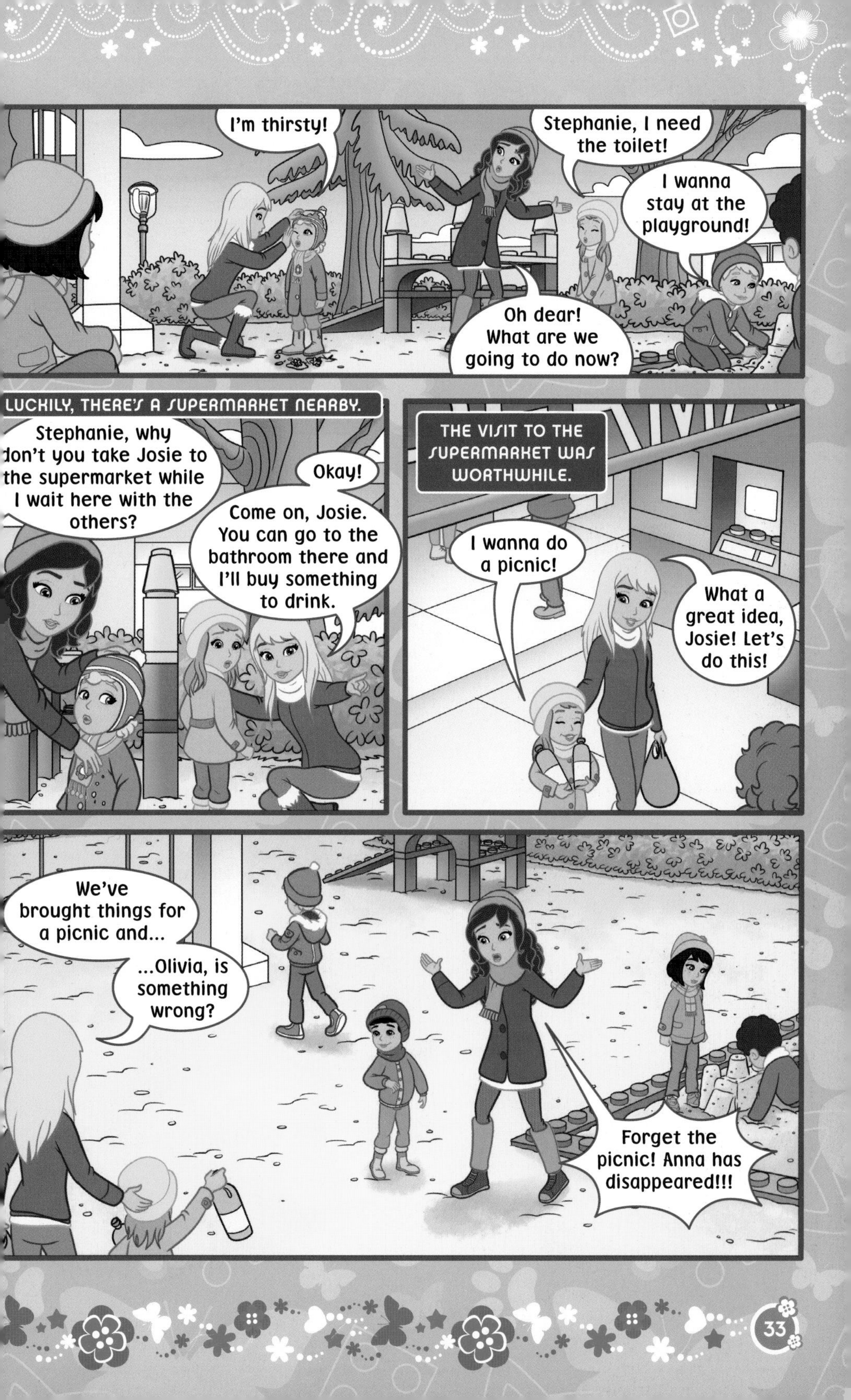
I'm thirsty!
Stephanie, I need the toilet!
I wanna stay at the playground!
Oh dear! What are we going to do now?
LUCKILY, THERE'S A SUPERMARKET NEARBY.
Stephanie, why don't you take Josie to the supermarket while I wait here with the others?
Okay!
Come on, Josie. You can go to the bathroom there and I'll buy something to drink.
THE VISIT TO THE SUPERMARKET WAS WORTHWHILE.
I wanna do a picnic!
What a great idea, Josie! Let's do this!
We've brought things for a picnic and...
...Olivia, is something wrong?
Forget the picnic! Anna has disappeared!!!

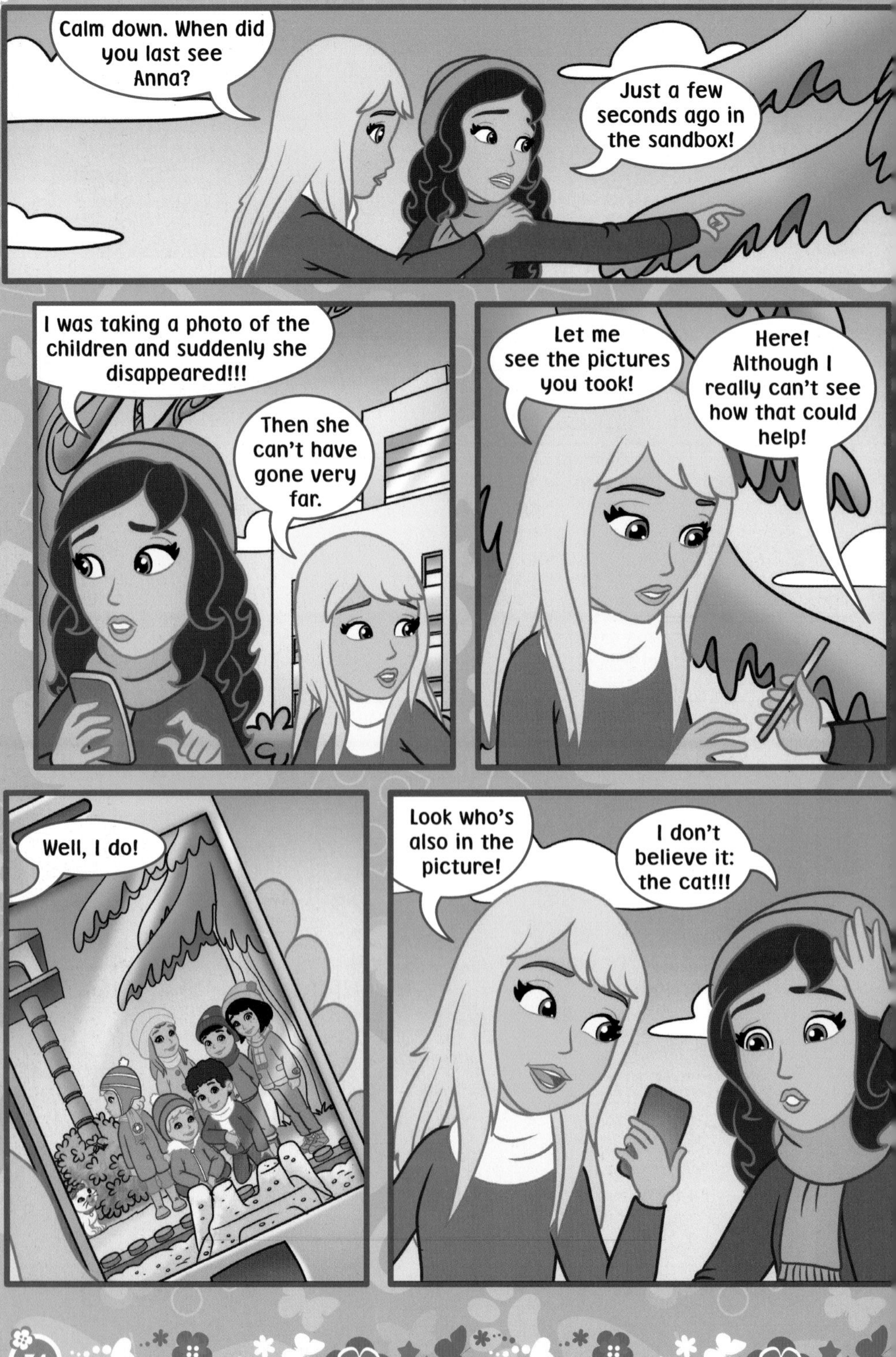
Calm down. When did you last see Anna?
Just a few seconds ago in the sandbox!
I was taking a photo of the children and suddenly she disappeared!!!
Then she can't have gone very far.
Let me see the pictures you took!
Here! Although I really can't see how that could help!
Well, I do!
Look who's also in the picture!
I don't believe it: the cat!!!

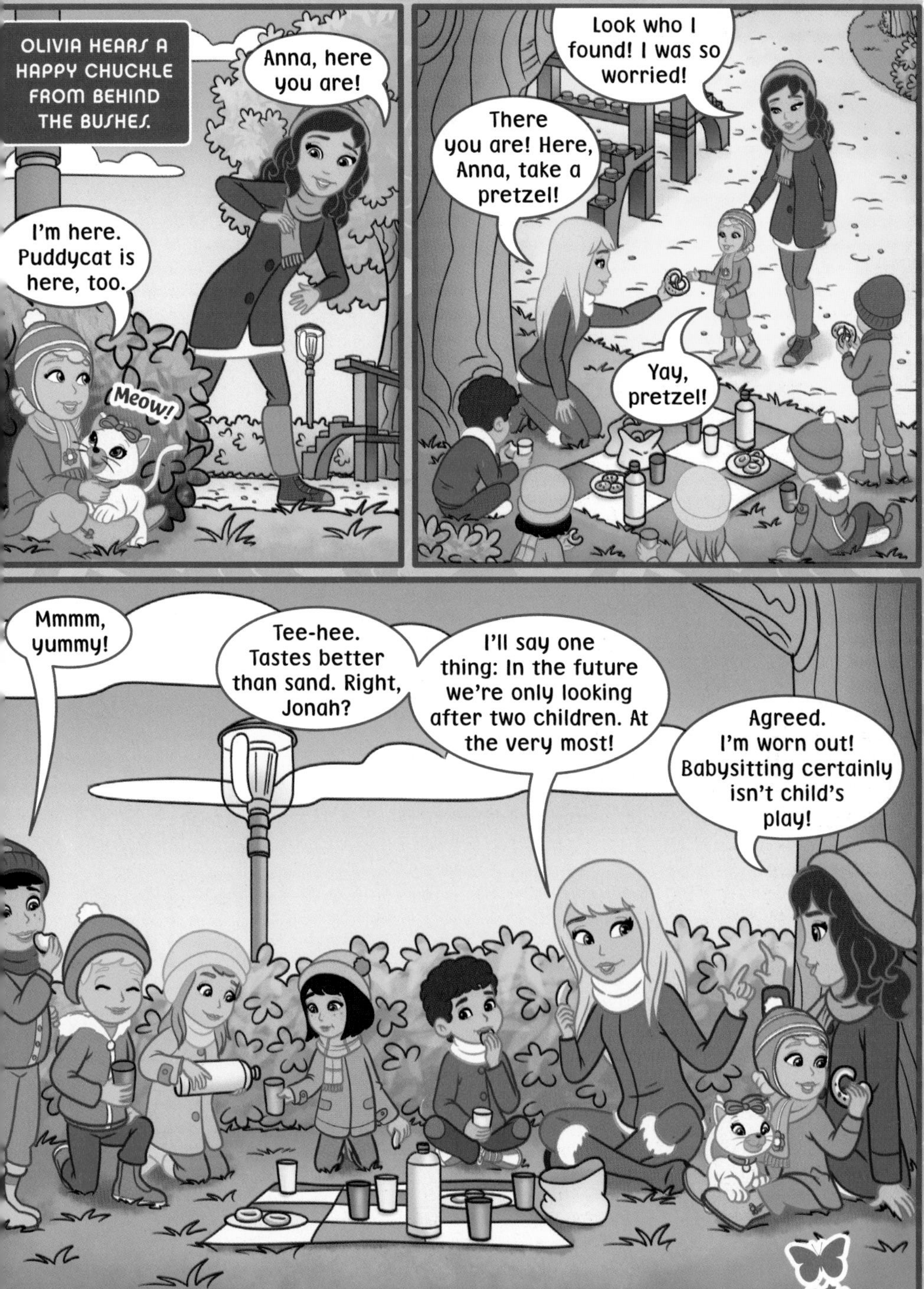
OLIVIA HEARS A HAPPY CHUCKLE FROM BEHIND THE BUSHES.
Anna, here you are!
I'm here. Puddycat is here, too.
Meow!
Look who I found! I was so worried!
There you are! Here, Anna, take a pretzel!
Yay, pretzel!
Mmmm, yummy!
Tee-hee. Tastes better than sand. Right, Jonah?
I'll say one thing: In the future we're only looking after two children. At the very most!
Agreed. I'm worn out! Babysitting certainly isn't child's play!
End

Want a Job?

Start Your Own Business!

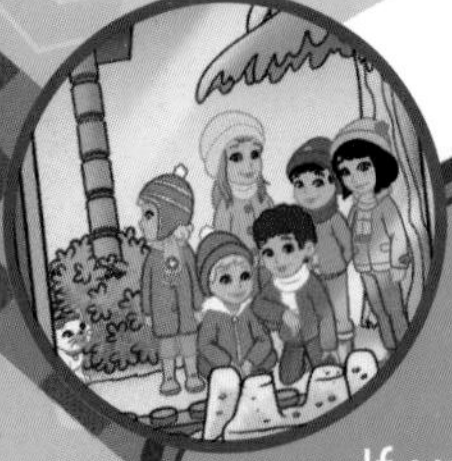

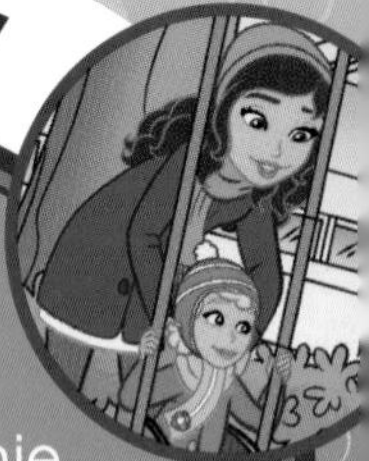

If you love kids as much as Olivia and Stephanie do, babysitting will be a great job for you—one day! Watching kids is a *huge* responsibility and a lot of work. For now, you'd probably have more fun building your skills by creating a small business. Just follow these steps to help you launch your first career today! (Make sure you talk to your parents first. Involving your guardians guarantees a safe and fun business!)

What's the Job?!

First, you should consider your interests. If you like pets, you could start walking dogs or feeding the neighbors' cats when they are out of town. If you like cooking, you could sell cookies or open a lemonade stand. If you like computers, you could teach your grandparents how to use e-mail. If you can't think of a business, maybe discuss it with your parents. You and one of your guardians or siblings could create a business together.

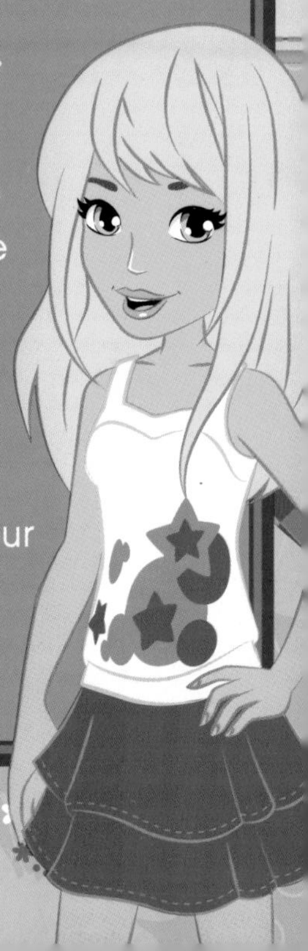

You Name It!

The name of your business is something you're going to use a lot, so it should be a name that you like! Pick something that's easy to understand and remember but also has a little flair. Try to choose something catchy. Write down some options and then ask your friends to vote on their faves! Here're a few that might be fun to try:

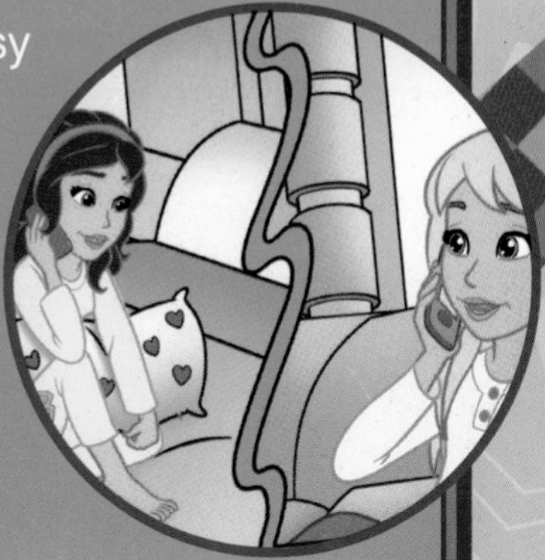

- **Dana's Dog-Walking Service**
- **Snack Time Stand—Lemonade and Cookies by Amy**
- **E-mail 101**
- **Melanie the Chore Helper!**

Got a Logo?

Most businesses have a logo or icon, which is an image people recognize as belonging to that business or product, like the recognizable red icon that represents LEGO. What do you want your logo to look like?

What's Your Business Motto?

It's your business, so what are the top five things you would want people who hire you to know about your service and what you offer? In other words, why should they hire YOU? Write down five things and make sure you tell people when they ask about your business. Check out the sample motto below:

- **"I am responsible, clean, helpful, organized, and thoughtful!"**

Spread the Word!

When you start a new business, you need to market it. When you "market" something, you are spreading the word about it so people know you're there. Jot down some ways you would market your new business! Who would you tell and how?

Hint #1: Think about the types of people who will be hiring you, and then figure out how you can best reach those people.

Hint #2: Don't market to strangers. It's better to stay close to home, and always make sure your guardians know where they can find you.

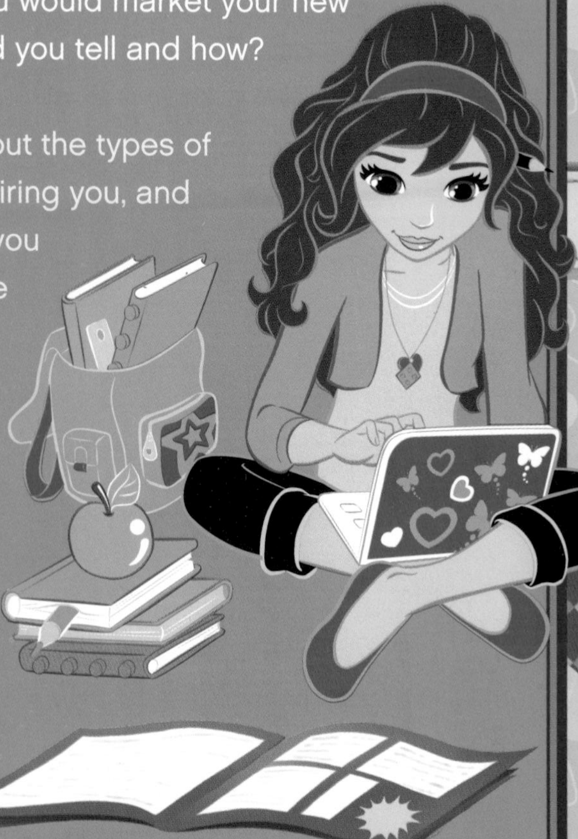

Here are some suggestions of people to market your business to:

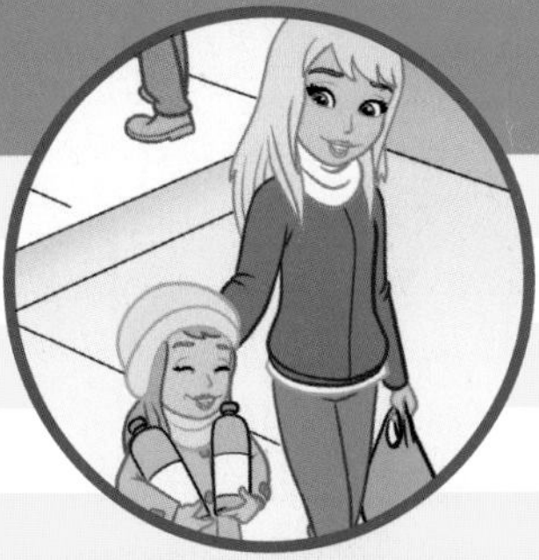

- Family and extended family
- Friends and friends' families
- Friends of your parents
- Neighbors
- Teachers

Design a Poster!

In order to spread the word about a business, many people design posters. When placed in your neighborhood or a community center, they can be seen by a lot of people. Remember not to give out your personal contact information. It is better for strangers to go through your parents or guardian. (Remember, it's always a good idea to involve an adult to keep yourself safe!)

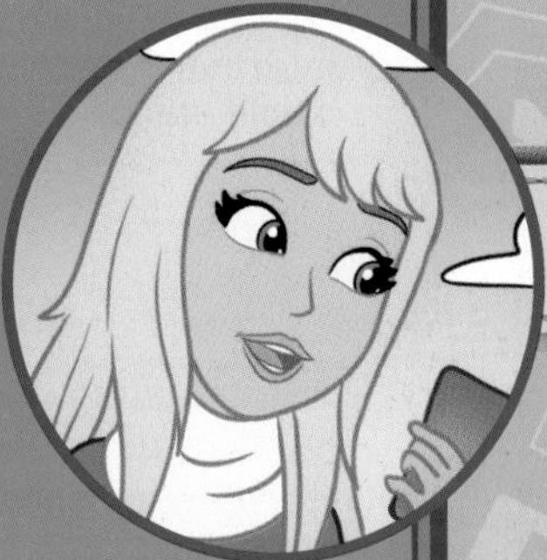

You can also make a digital "flyer" and send it to your friends and family in an e-mail blast.

What would your first poster look like? Some information to include:

- The name of your service
- How to contact you
- What you charge for your service
- When your service is available

Enchanting Penguins

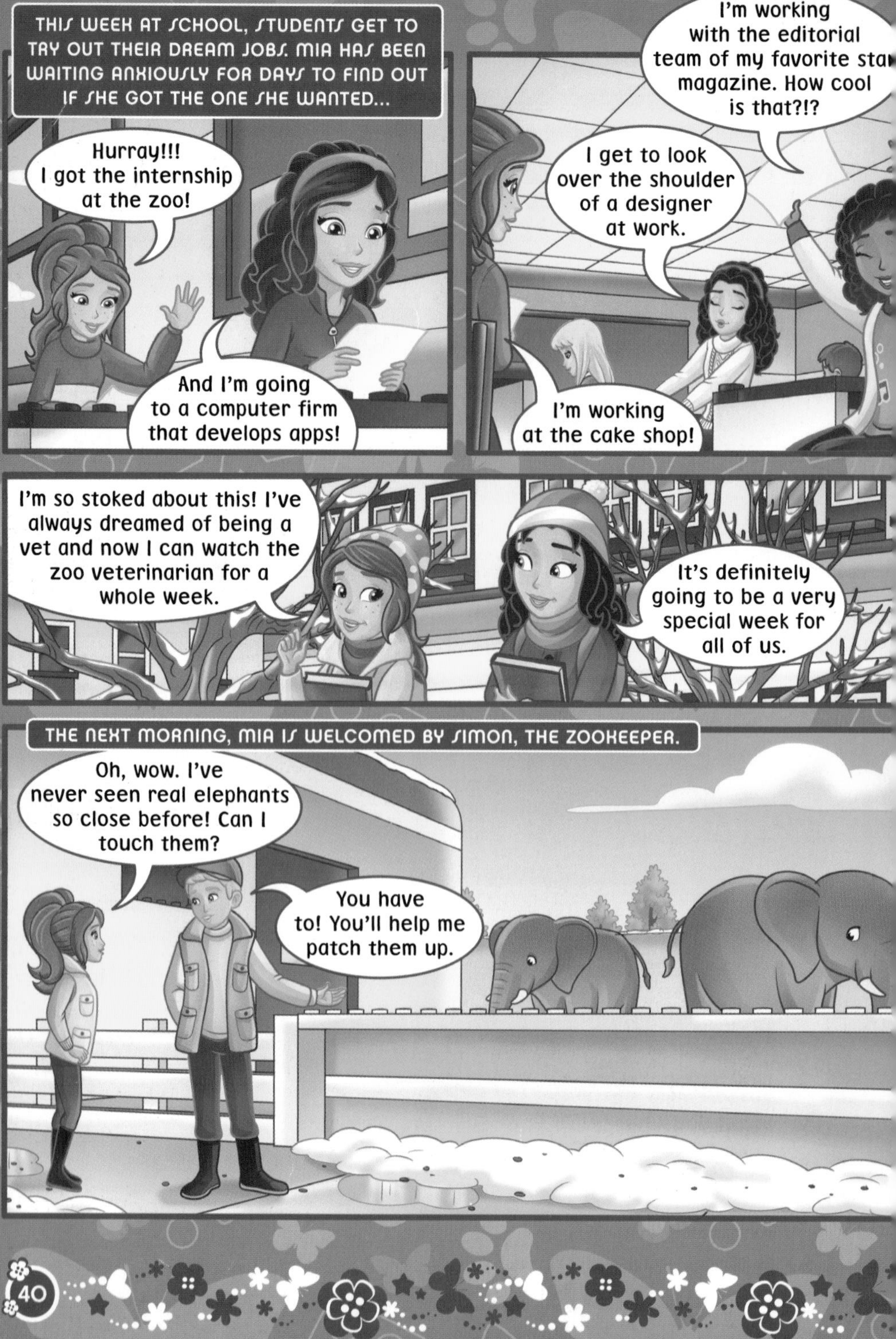
THIS WEEK AT SCHOOL, STUDENTS GET TO TRY OUT THEIR DREAM JOBS. MIA HAS BEEN WAITING ANXIOUSLY FOR DAYS TO FIND OUT IF SHE GOT THE ONE SHE WANTED...
Hurray!!! I got the internship at the zoo!
And I'm going to a computer firm that develops apps!
I'm working with the editorial team of my favorite sta magazine. How cool is that?!?
I get to look over the shoulder of a designer at work.
I'm working at the cake shop!
I'm so stoked about this! I've always dreamed of being a vet and now I can watch the zoo veterinarian for a whole week.
It's definitely going to be a very special week for all of us.
THE NEXT MORNING, MIA IS WELCOMED BY SIMON, THE ZOOKEEPER.
Oh, wow. I've never seen real elephants so close before! Can I touch them?
You have to! You'll help me patch them up.

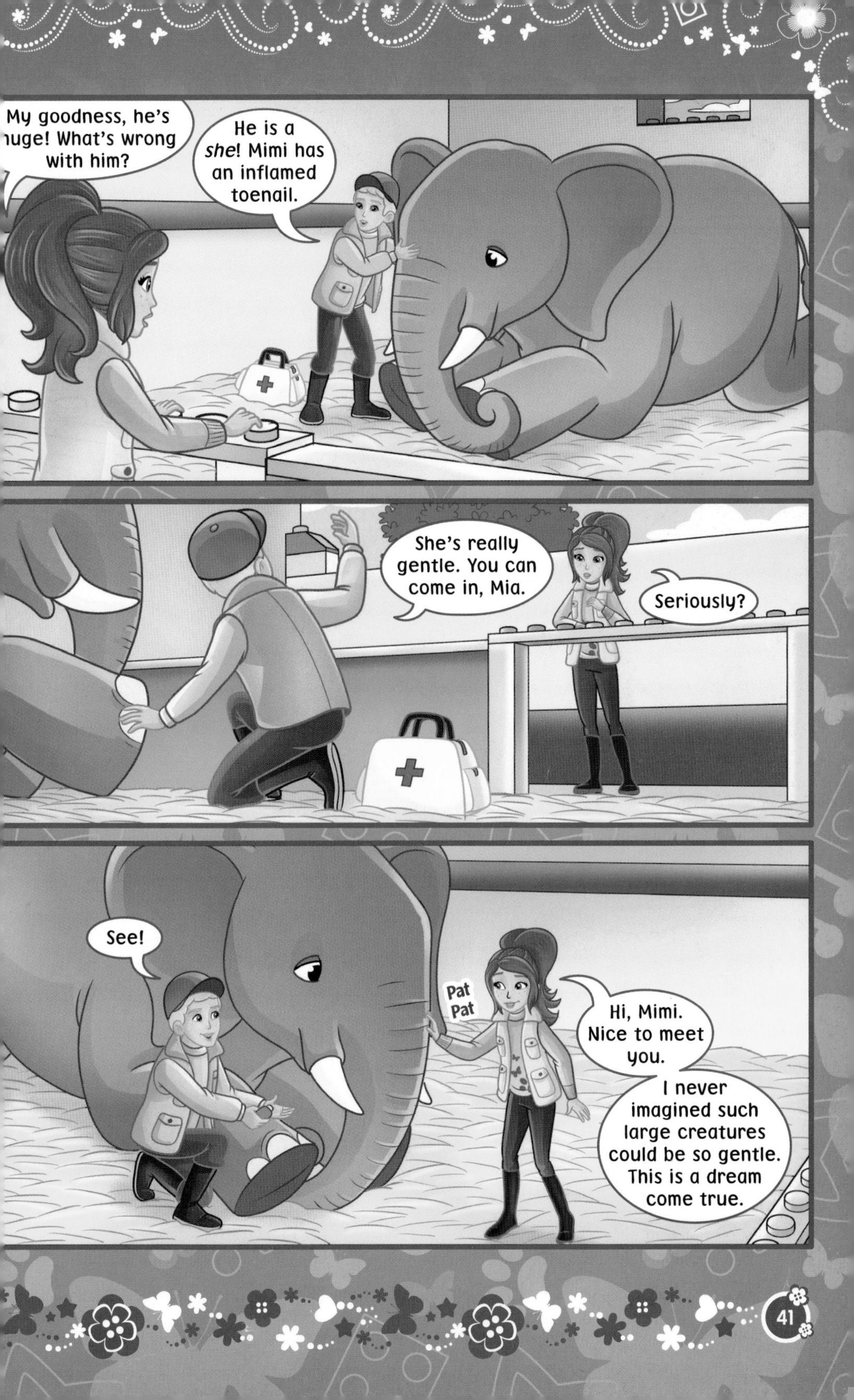
My goodness, he's uge! What's wrong with him?
He is a *she*! Mimi has an inflamed toenail.
She's really gentle. You can come in, Mia.
Seriously?
See!
Pat Pat
Hi, Mimi. Nice to meet you.
I never imagined such large creatures could be so gentle. This is a dream come true.

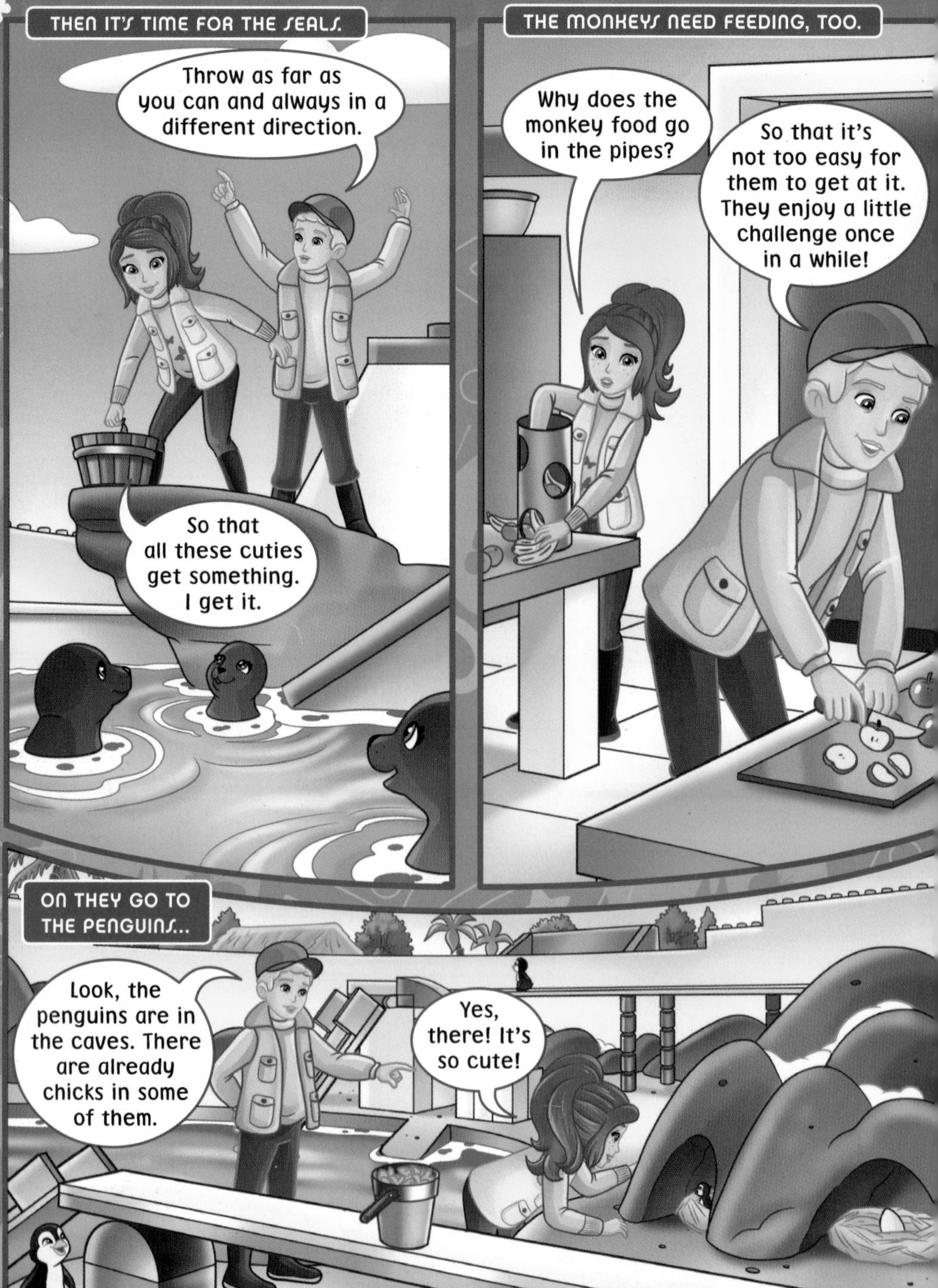
THEN IT'S TIME FOR THE SEALS.
Throw as far as you can and always in a different direction.
So that all these cuties get something. I get it.
THE MONKEYS NEED FEEDING, TOO.
Why does the monkey food go in the pipes?
So that it's not too easy for them to get at it. They enjoy a little challenge once in a while!
ON THEY GO TO THE PENGUINS...
Look, the penguins are in the caves. There are already chicks in some of them.
Yes, there! It's so cute!

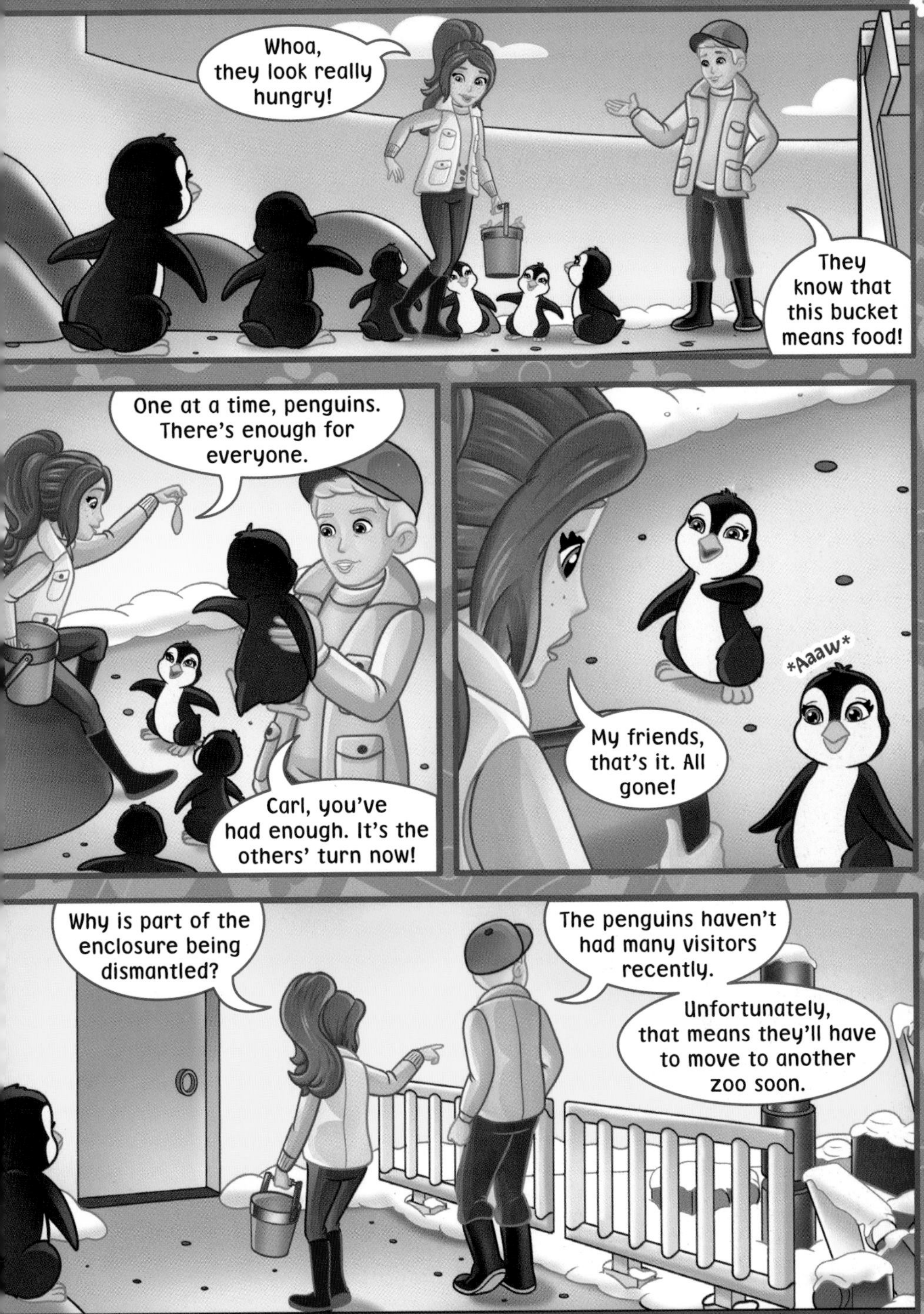
Whoa, they look really hungry!
They know that this bucket means food!
One at a time, penguins. There's enough for everyone.
Carl, you've had enough. It's the others' turn now!
Aaaw
My friends, that's it. All gone!
Why is part of the enclosure being dismantled?
The penguins haven't had many visitors recently.
Unfortunately, that means they'll have to move to another zoo soon.

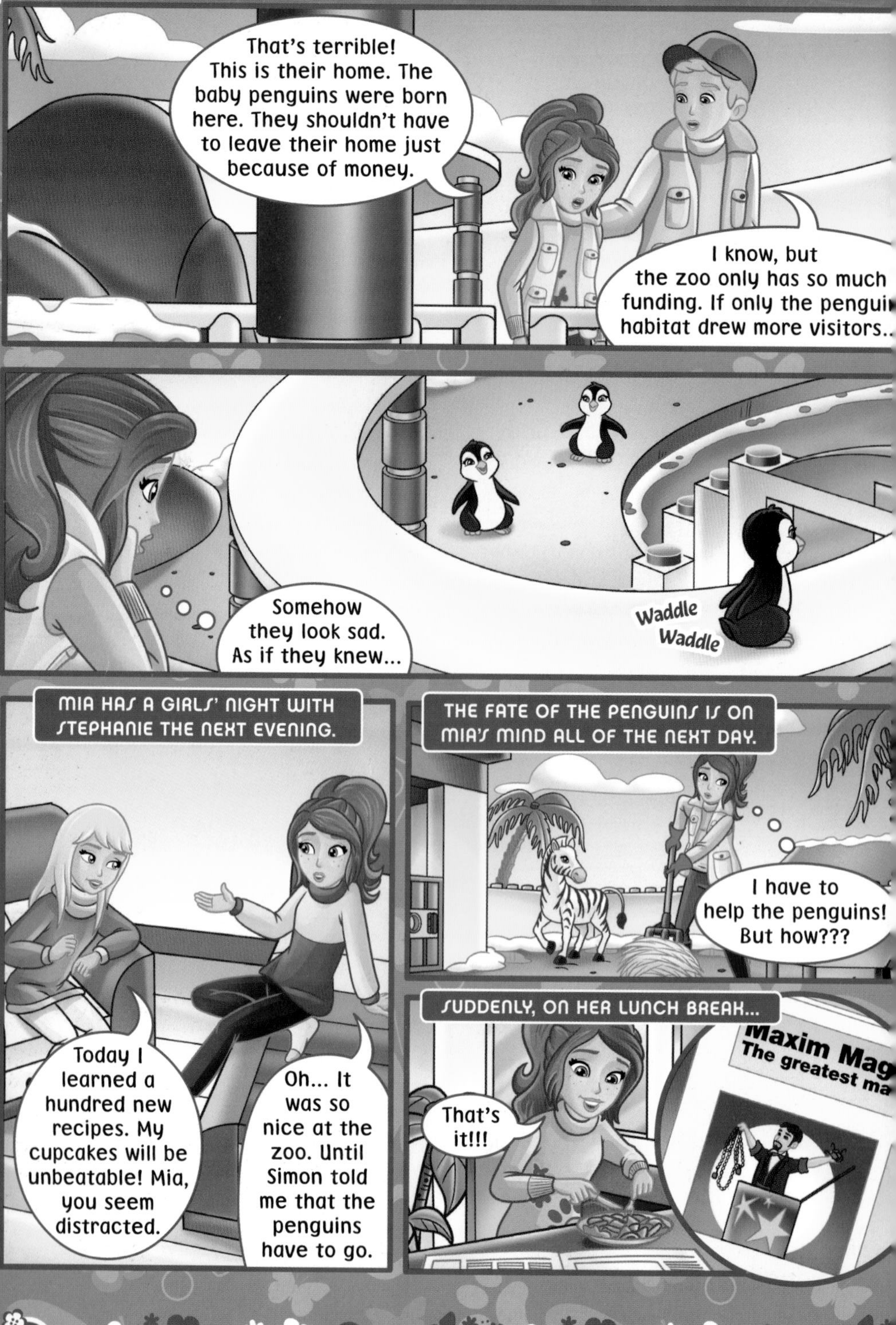
That's terrible! This is their home. The baby penguins were born here. They shouldn't have to leave their home just because of money.
I know, but the zoo only has so much funding. If only the pengui habitat drew more visitors..
Somehow they look sad. As if they knew...
Waddle Waddle
MIA HAS A GIRLS' NIGHT WITH STEPHANIE THE NEXT EVENING.
Today I learned a hundred new recipes. My cupcakes will be unbeatable! Mia, you seem distracted.
Oh... It was so nice at the zoo. Until Simon told me that the penguins have to go.
THE FATE OF THE PENGUINS IS ON MIA'S MIND ALL OF THE NEXT DAY.
I have to help the penguins! But how???
SUDDENLY, ON HER LUNCH BREAK...
That's it!!!
Maxim Mag
The greatest ma

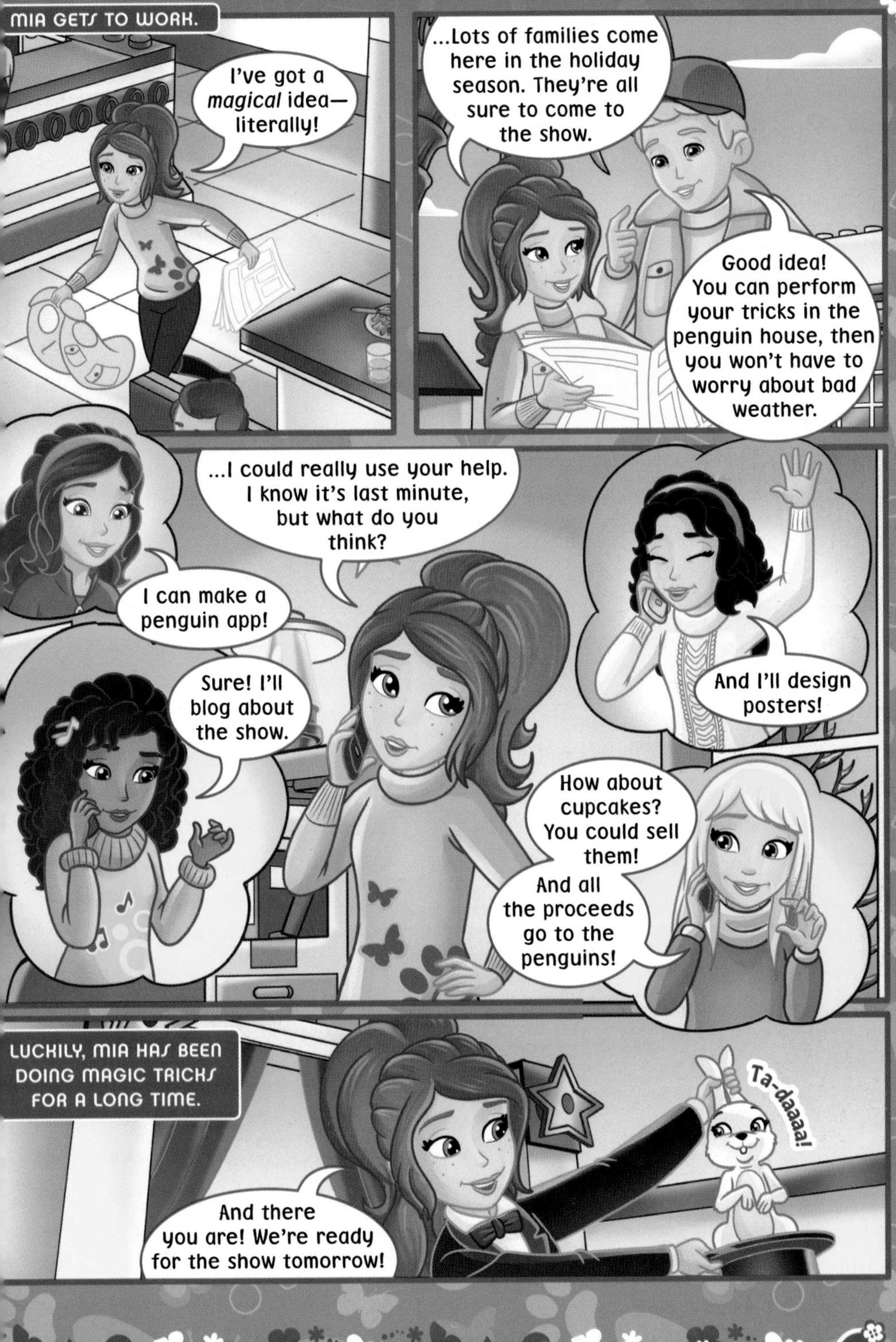
MIA GETS TO WORK.
I've got a *magical* idea—literally!
...Lots of families come here in the holiday season. They're all sure to come to the show.
Good idea! You can perform your tricks in the penguin house, then you won't have to worry about bad weather.
...I could really use your help. I know it's last minute, but what do you think?
I can make a penguin app!
And I'll design posters!
Sure! I'll blog about the show.
How about cupcakes? You could sell them!
And all the proceeds go to the penguins!
LUCKILY, MIA HAS BEEN DOING MAGIC TRICKS FOR A LONG TIME.
Ta-daaaa!
And there you are! We're ready for the show tomorrow!

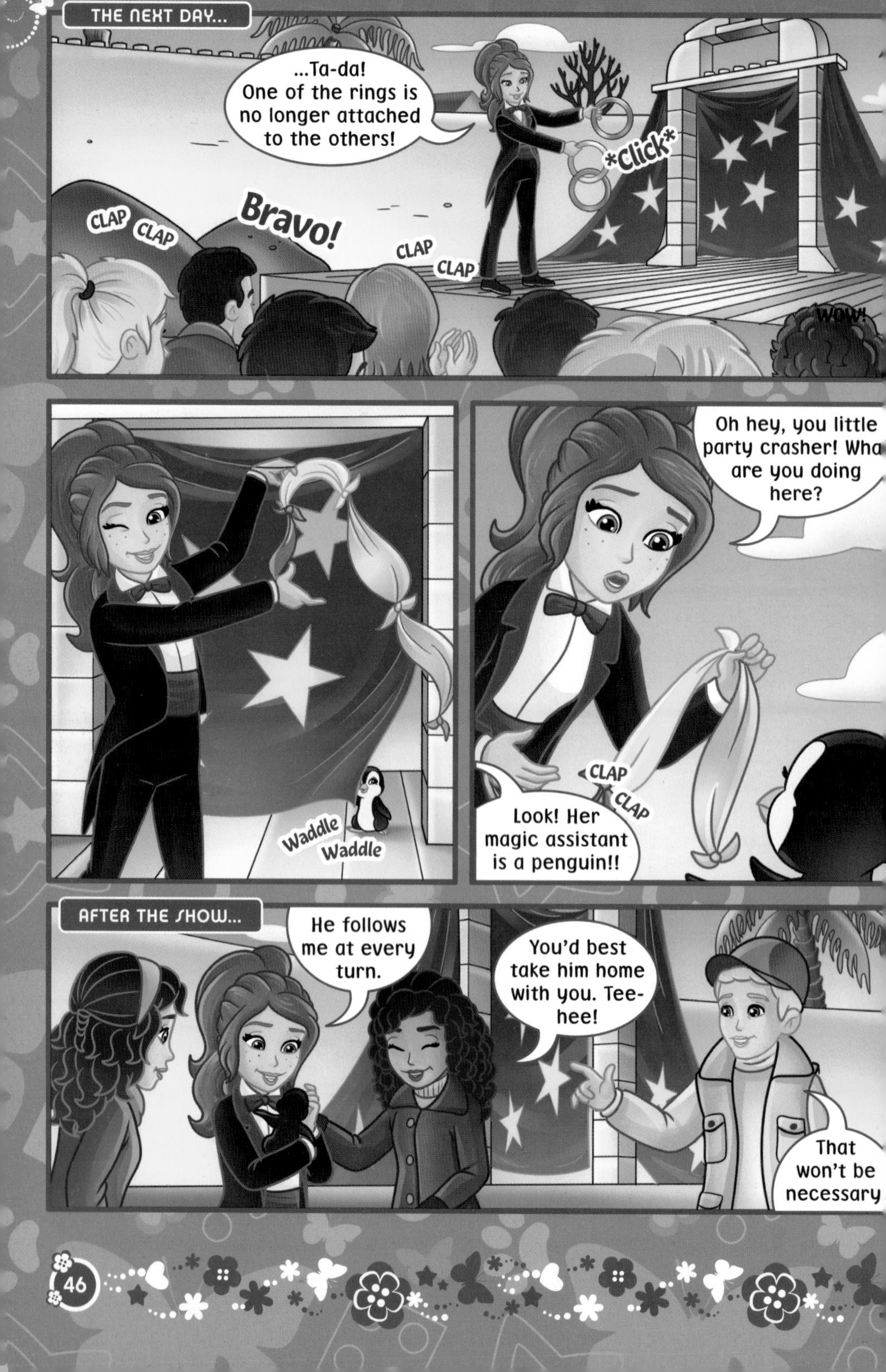
THE NEXT DAY...
...Ta-da! One of the rings is no longer attached to the others!
Click
CLAP CLAP
Bravo!
CLAP CLAP
WOW!
Waddle Waddle
Oh hey, you little party crasher! Wha are you doing here?
CLAP CLAP
Look! Her magic assistant is a penguin!!
AFTER THE SHOW...
He follows me at every turn.
You'd best take him home with you. Tee-hee!
That won't be necessary

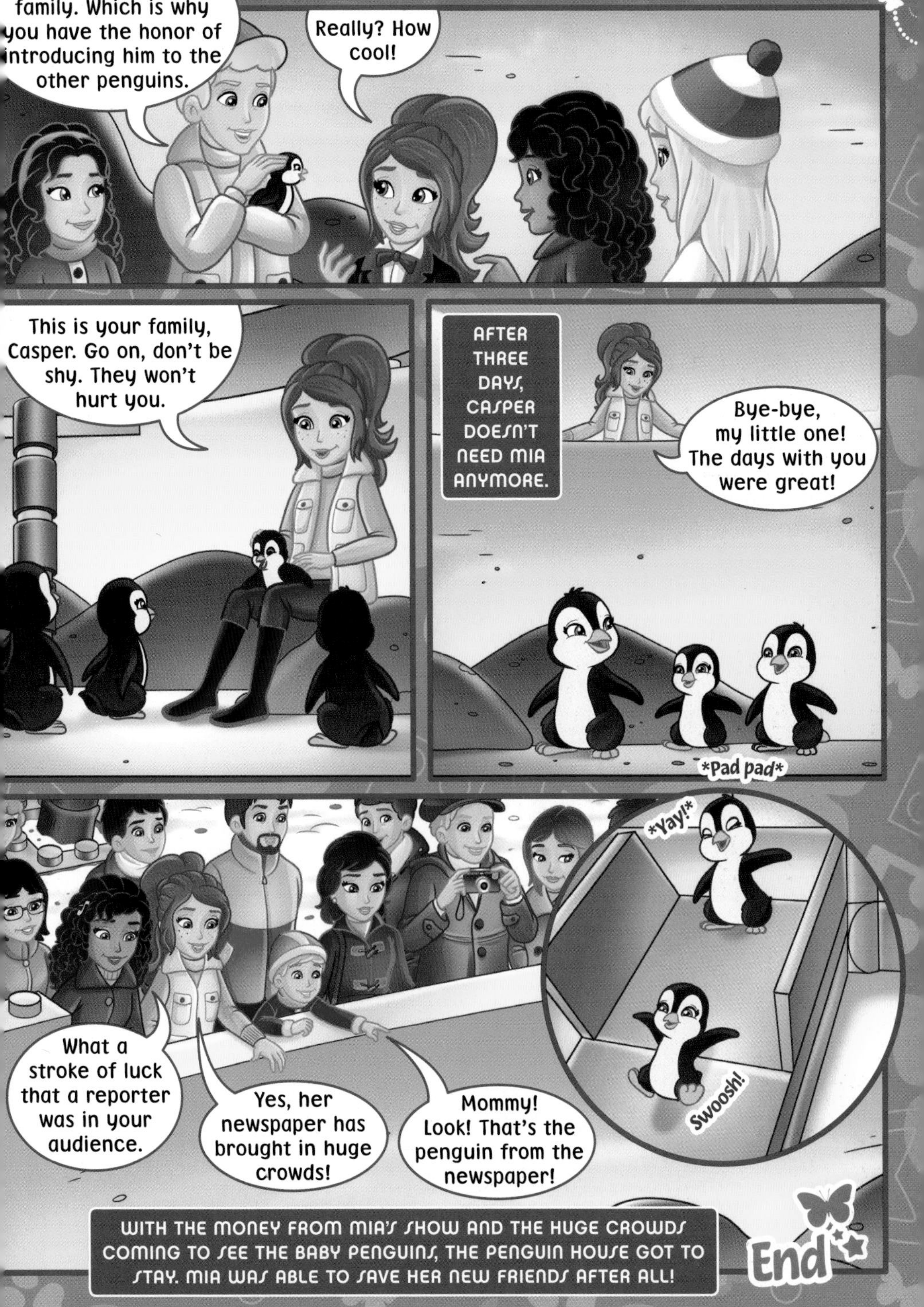
Casper seems to think you're his family. Which is why you have the honor of introducing him to the other penguins.
Really? How cool!
This is your family, Casper. Go on, don't be shy. They won't hurt you.
AFTER THREE DAYS, CASPER DOESN'T NEED MIA ANYMORE.
Bye-bye, my little one! The days with you were great!
Pad pad
Yay!
Swoosh!
What a stroke of luck that a reporter was in your audience.
Yes, her newspaper has brought in huge crowds!
Mommy! Look! That's the penguin from the newspaper!
WITH THE MONEY FROM MIA'S SHOW AND THE HUGE CROWDS COMING TO SEE THE BABY PENGUINS, THE PENGUIN HOUSE GOT TO STAY. MIA WAS ABLE TO SAVE HER NEW FRIENDS AFTER ALL!
End

Meet Jane Goodall

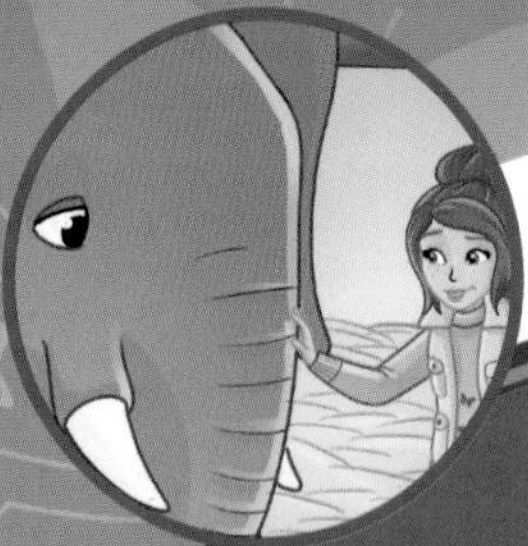

Animal Researcher

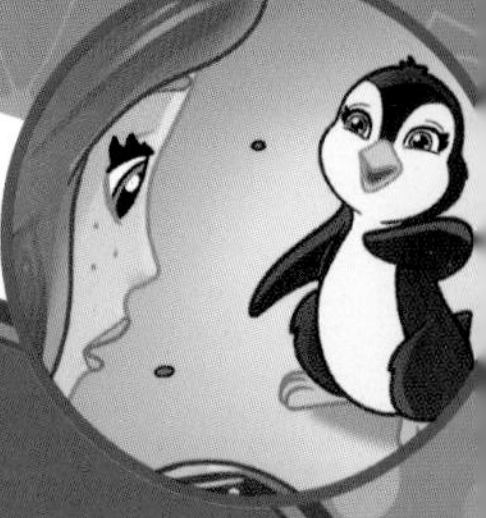

Mia isn't the first girl to dream of working with animals. One young girl who dreamed of working with chimpanzees from a very young age not only grew up to live out her dream but also became one of the world's most famous animal researchers!

Jane Goodall was born on April 3, 1934, in London, England. When she was only one year old, Jane received a stuffed animal chimpanzee from her father that she named Jubilee and carried with her everywhere. At a young age, she realized her love for animals and her desire to work with chimpanzees in particular. At the age of twenty-three, Jane moved to Africa to study chimpanzees in the wild!

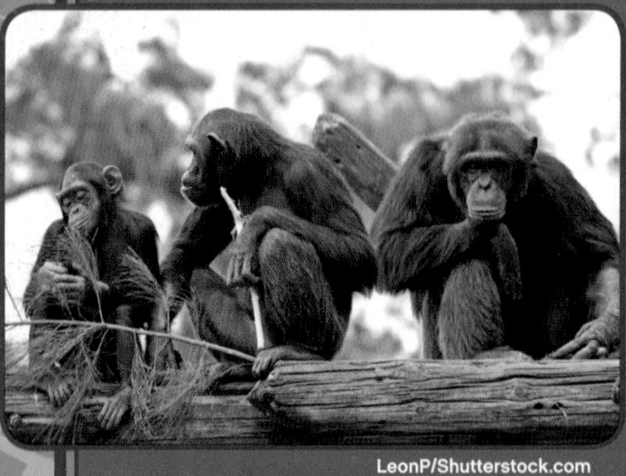

LeonP/Shutterstock.com

This was a long time ago, so not much was known about how chimpanzees behaved or interacted with one another in their own habitats. When Jane went to live on the farm of a friend in the Kenya highlands, it soon led her to venture into the forests of Tanzania to study the chimpanzees firsthand. Scientists thought that humans were the only species to make tools for certain things like eating, building, or gathering food. Jane discovered on one of her visits to the forest that the chimpanzees were doing just that—they made tools out of tree branches for fishing insects out of holes!

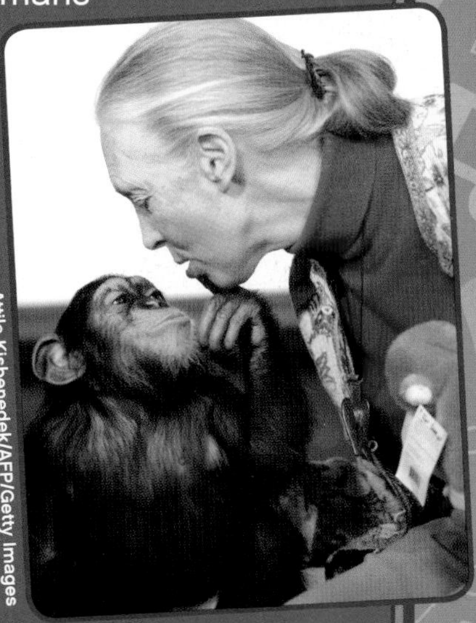
Attila Kisbenedek/AFP/Getty Images

Another important discovery made by Jane was that chimpanzees weren't actually vegetarians like most scientists thought. Instead, they ate small animals. She also observed that they had a basic language that they used to communicate, which was made up of about twenty different sounds. Jane worked with chimpanzees her whole life, and in her later years became known throughout the world for her expertise.

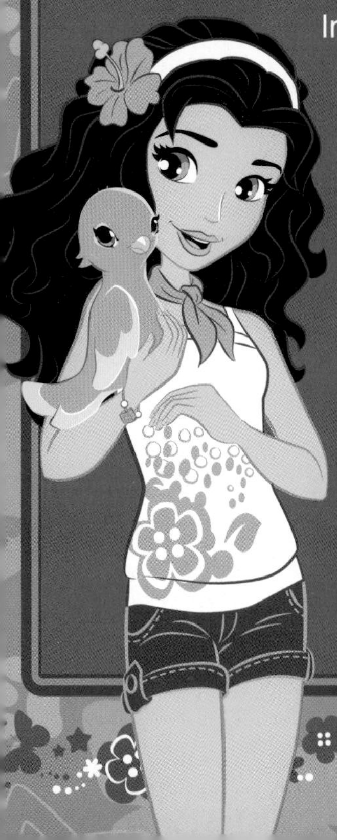

If you love animals as much as Jane did, go learn more about all the different kinds of animal professions you can have one day!

Trip to Winter Wonderland

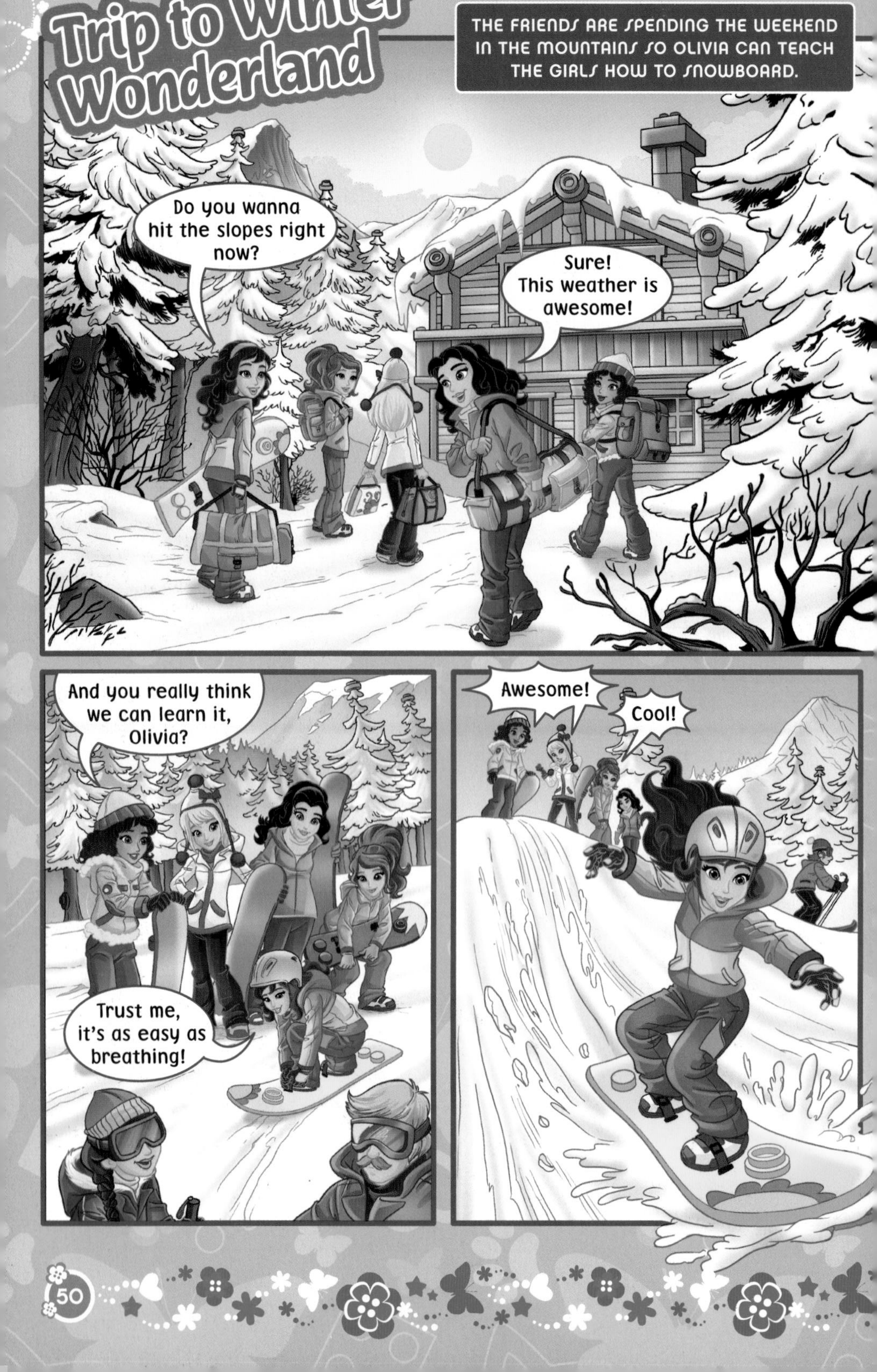
THE FRIENDS ARE SPENDING THE WEEKEND IN THE MOUNTAINS SO OLIVIA CAN TEACH THE GIRLS HOW TO SNOWBOARD.
Do you wanna hit the slopes right now?
Sure! This weather is awesome!
And you really think we can learn it, Olivia?
Trust me, it's as easy as breathing!
Awesome!
Cool!

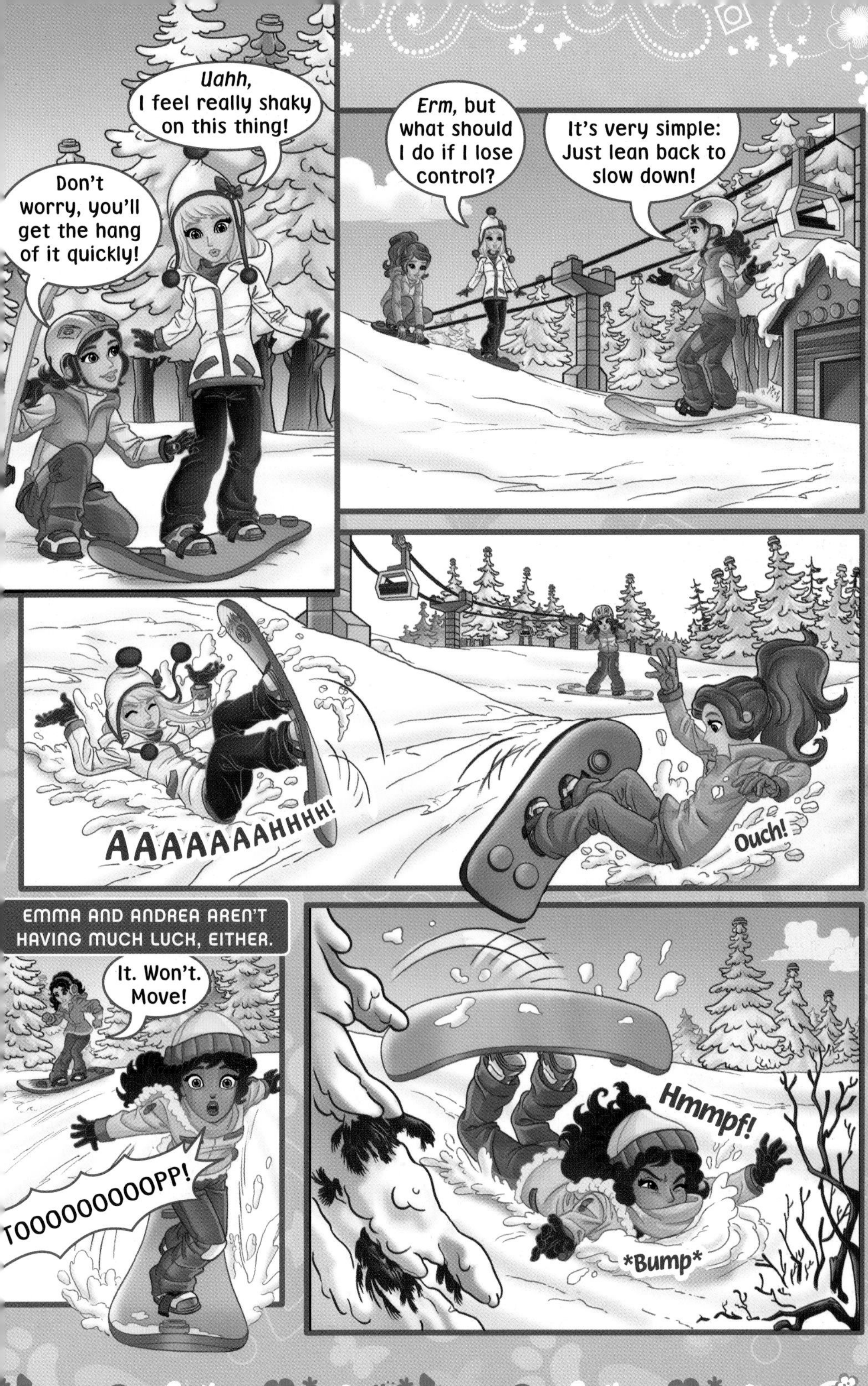

Uahh, I feel really shaky on this thing!
Don't worry, you'll get the hang of it quickly!
Erm, but what should I do if I lose control?
It's very simple: Just lean back to slow down!
AAAAAAAHHHH!
Ouch!
EMMA AND ANDREA AREN'T HAVING MUCH LUCK, EITHER.
It. Won't. Move!
TOOOOOOOOOPP!
Hmmpf!
Bump

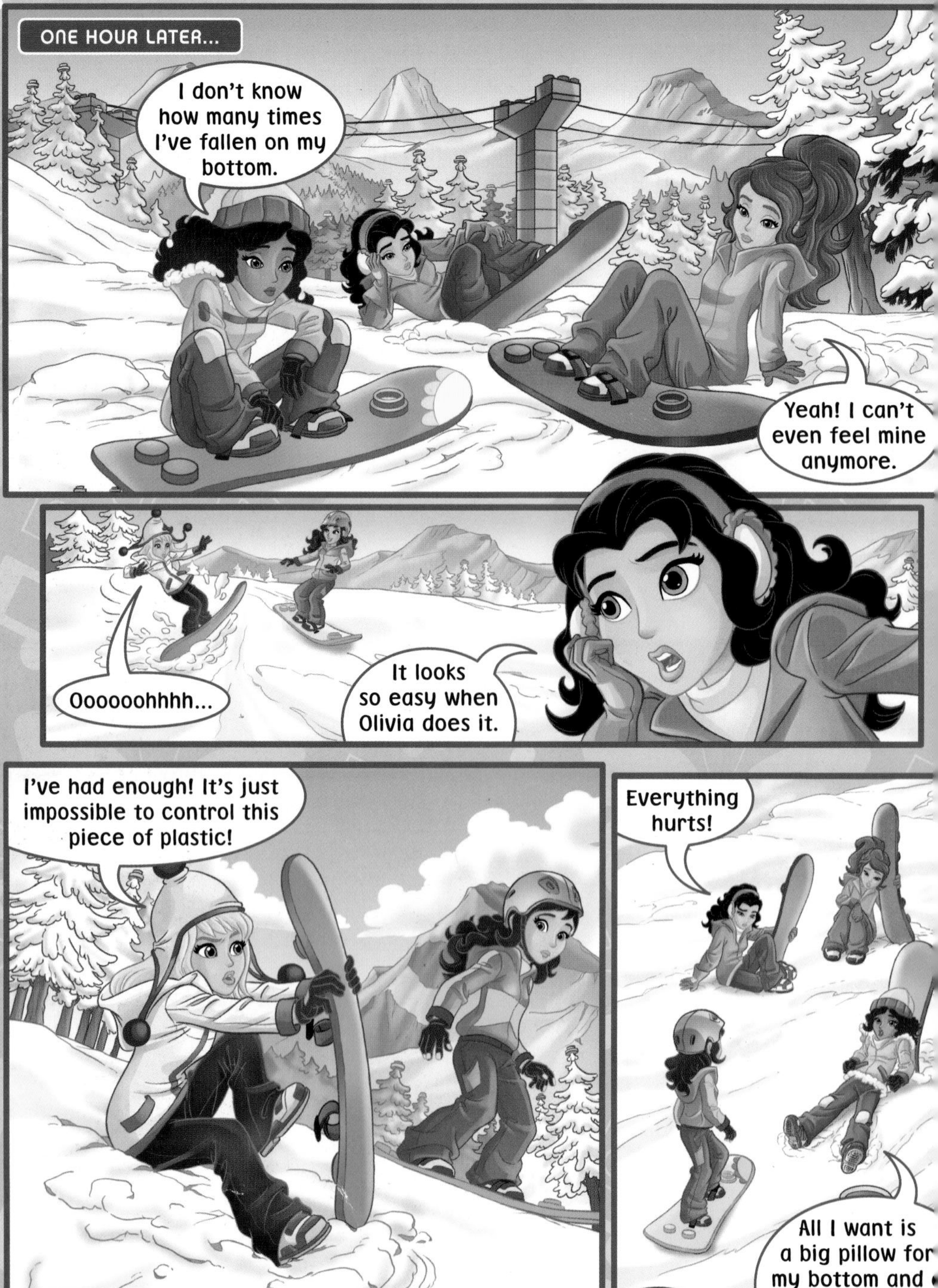

ONE HOUR LATER...
I don't know how many times I've fallen on my bottom.
Yeah! I can't even feel mine anymore.
Oooooohhhh...
It looks so easy when Olivia does it.
I've had enough! It's just impossible to control this piece of plastic!
Everything hurts!
All I want is a big pillow for my bottom and hot chocolate!

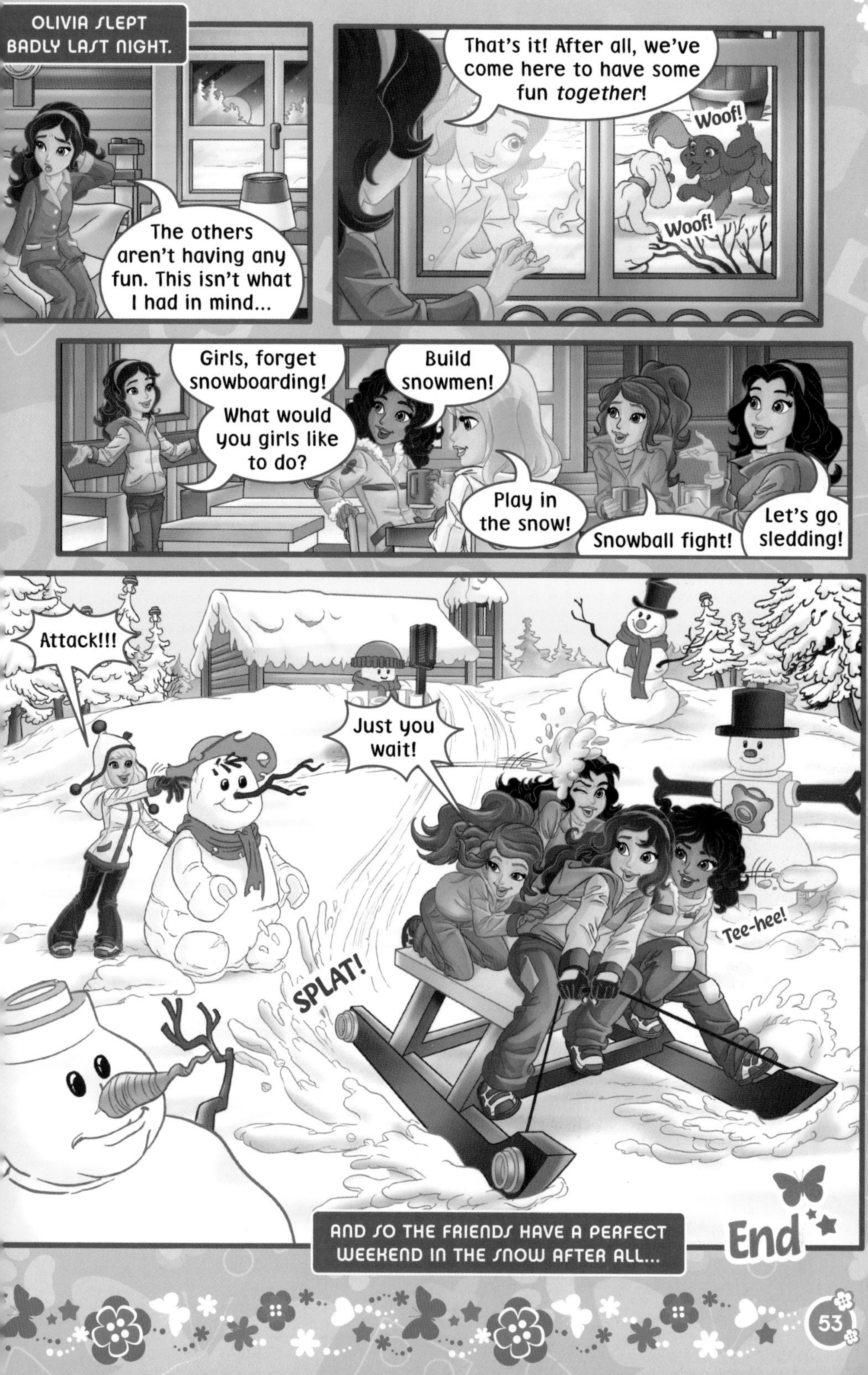
OLIVIA SLEPT BADLY LAST NIGHT.
The others aren't having any fun. This isn't what I had in mind...
That's it! After all, we've come here to have some fun *together*!
Woof!
Woof!
Girls, forget snowboarding!
What would you girls like to do?
Build snowmen!
Play in the snow!
Snowball fight!
Let's go sledding!
Attack!!!
Just you wait!
SPLAT!
Tee-hee!
AND SO THE FRIENDS HAVE A PERFECT WEEKEND IN THE SNOW AFTER ALL...
End

Fun with Friends!

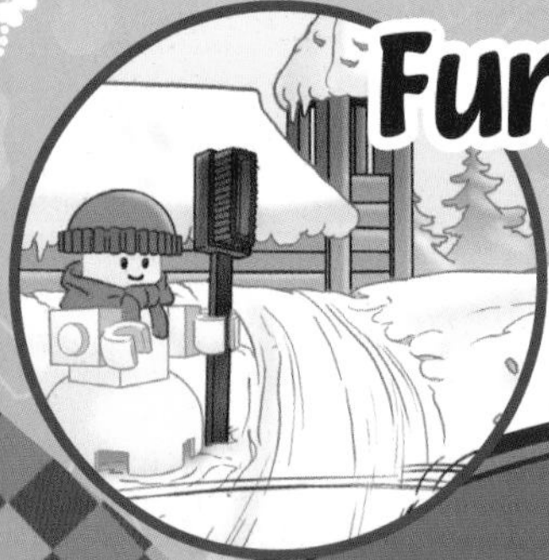

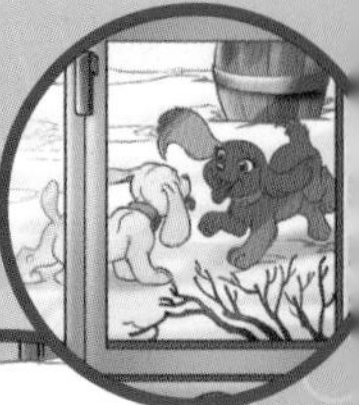

Snowed In?!

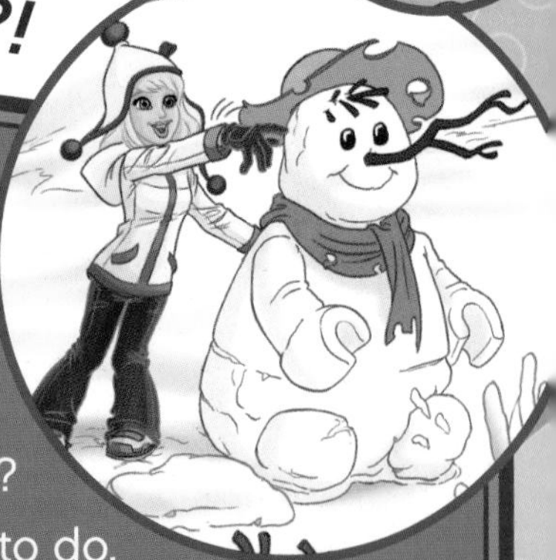

The LEGO Friends had great weather for snowboarding, but have you ever been snowed (or rained) in? It can feel like you have nothing fun to do. But here are a few entertaining ways to pass the time indoors with your best friends!

It's a Sing-Off!

Sit in a circle and go around it clockwise or counter-clockwise. The first person starts singing a song, and the person next to her needs to listen for a word or phrase in the song's lyrics that she knows exists in the lyrics of a different song. Once she hears that word or phrase, she jumps in and begins to sing a new song. If she can't think of something before the first person finishes her song, she's out! Keep going around the circle until there's a winner!

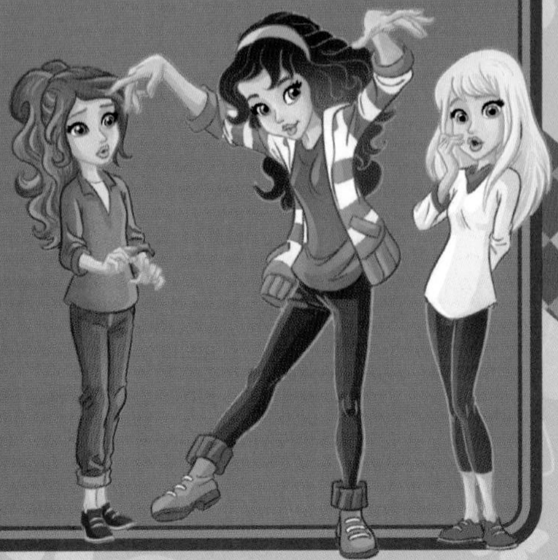

Screen Test

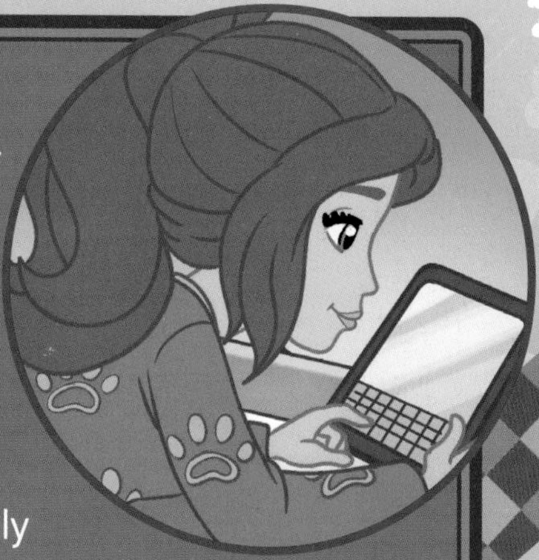

Write the names of your favorite movies or TV shows on pieces of paper, fold them in half, and then put them in a hat and mix them up. The first person will pick a piece of paper randomly and then has to act out a scene from the movie or show for her friends! Whoever guesses the correct answer goes next. Then she picks a new movie or show from the hat and acts out a new scene. You can also change the category to favorite songs, animals, or celebrities!

Build It!

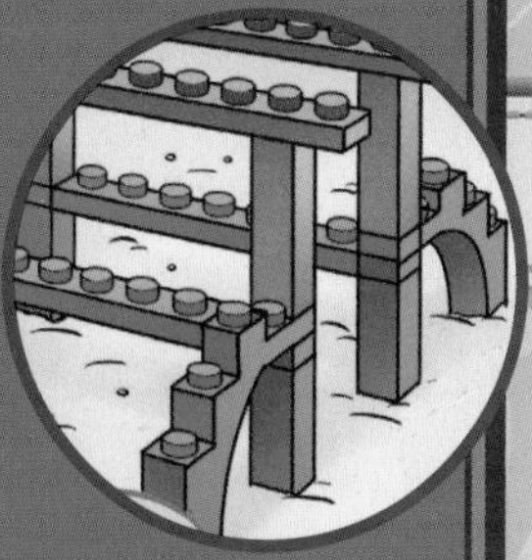

Grab your LEGO bricks and challenge one another to some building games! Use a stopwatch to time one another and see who can build the fastest LEGO Friends set from the instructions. Or everyone study a small LEGO build for thirty seconds, and then hide it. Now try to build it from memory. A third fun game using your LEGO sets would be to give everyone a blindfold and have them build something without using their eyes! It's not easy!

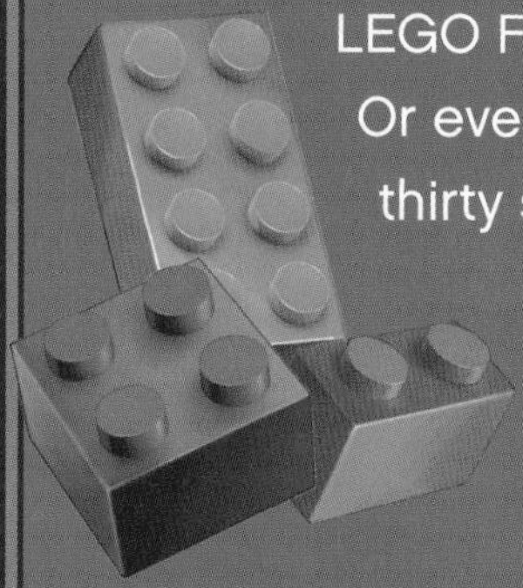

Girl Talk

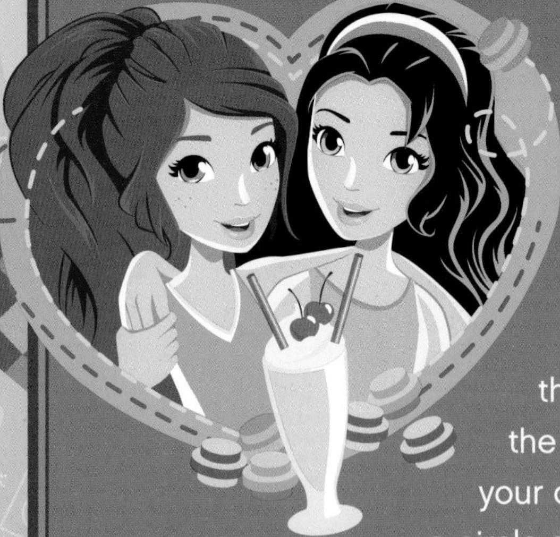

Sure, you talk to your friends all the time, but have you ever wanted to share something really special with them and not found the right moment? Here's your chance! Go around in a circle and share a secret that you've never shared before and see how much closer together it brings you.

Write a Story!

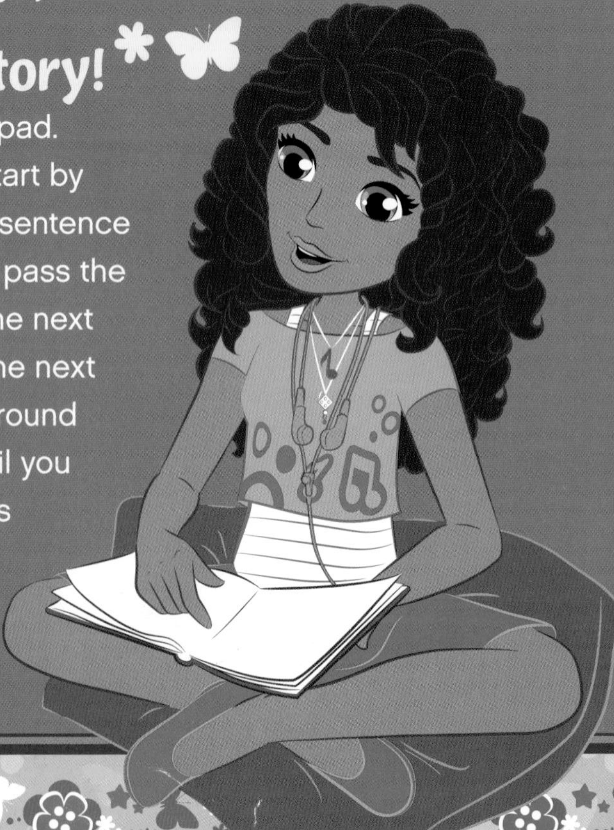

Grab a notepad. Someone will start by writing the first sentence of a story. They pass the notepad, and the next person writes the next sentence. Go around and around until you and your friends have created a story. Now, read it aloud.

It's All About Fun!

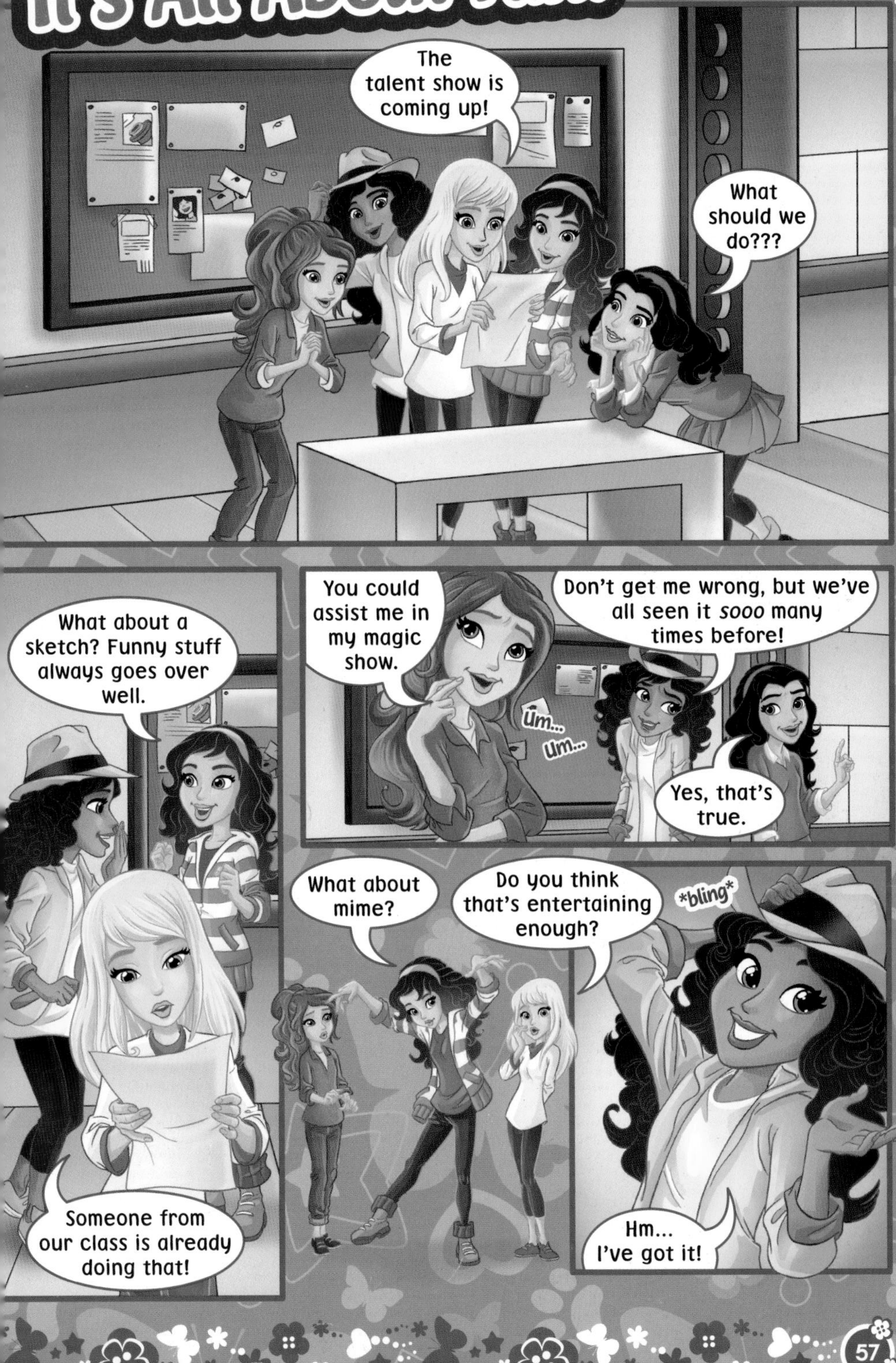

The talent show is coming up!
What should we do???
What about a sketch? Funny stuff always goes over well.
Someone from our class is already doing that!
You could assist me in my magic show.
Um...
Um...
Don't get me wrong, but we've all seen it *sooo* many times before!
Yes, that's true.
What about mime?
Do you think that's entertaining enough?
bling
Hm... I've got it!

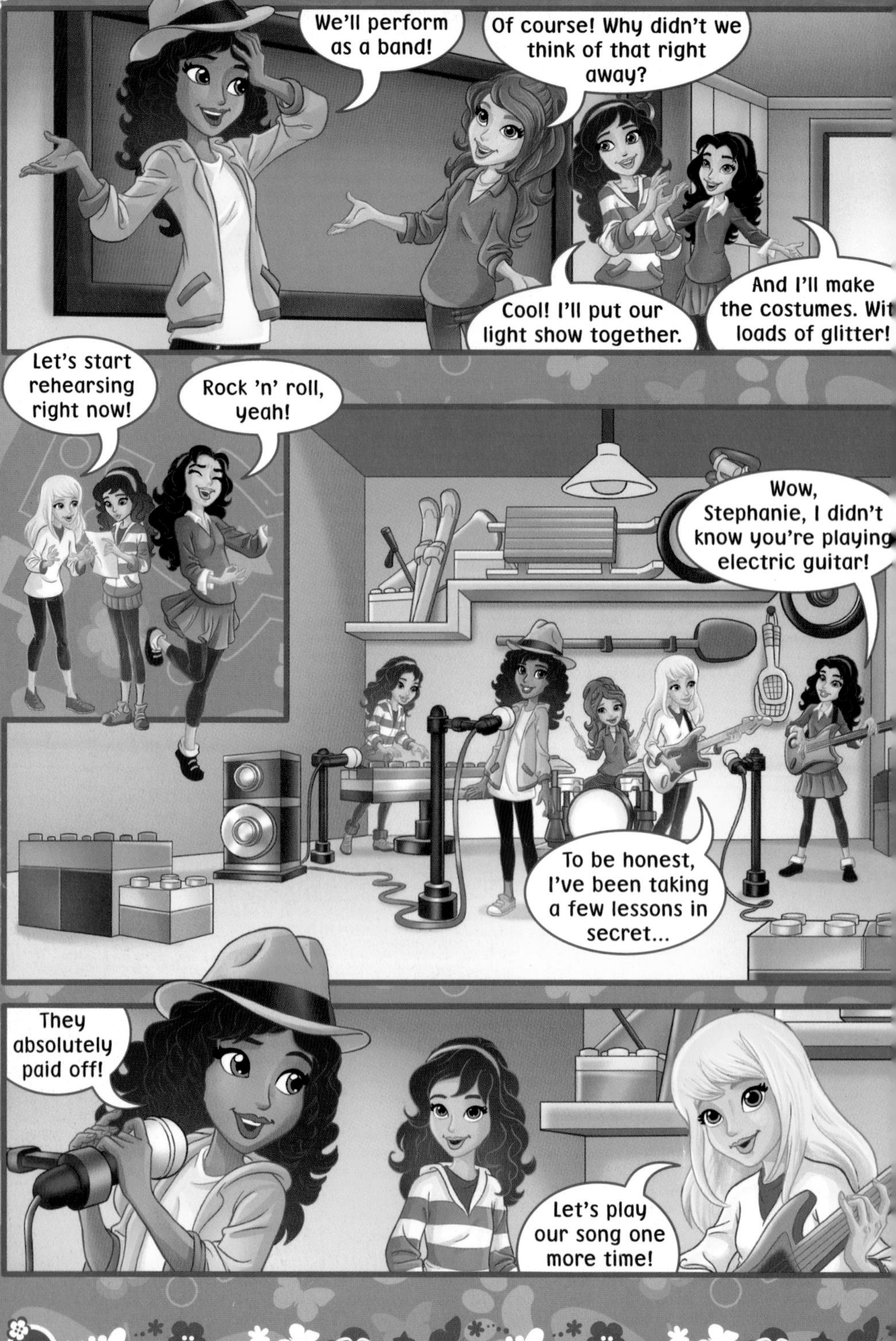
We'll perform as a band!
Of course! Why didn't we think of that right away?
Cool! I'll put our light show together.
And I'll make the costumes. Wit loads of glitter!
Let's start rehearsing right now!
Rock 'n' roll, yeah!
Wow, Stephanie, I didn't know you're playing electric guitar!
To be honest, I've been taking a few lessons in secret...
They absolutely paid off!
Let's play our song one more time!

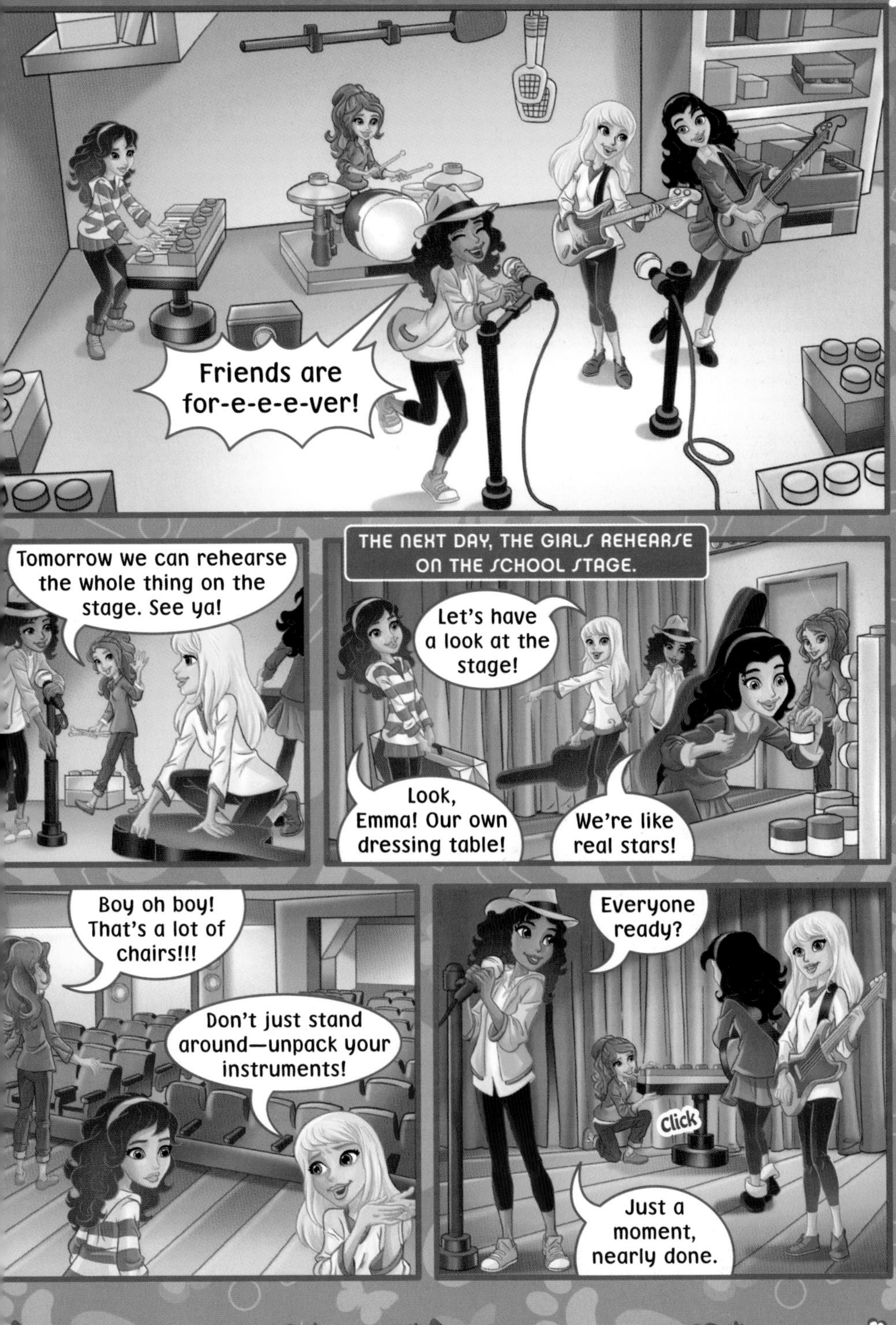
Friends are for-e-e-e-ver!
Tomorrow we can rehearse the whole thing on the stage. See ya!
THE NEXT DAY, THE GIRLS REHEARSE ON THE SCHOOL STAGE.
Let's have a look at the stage!
Look, Emma! Our own dressing table!
We're like real stars!
Boy oh boy! That's a lot of chairs!!!
Don't just stand around—unpack your instruments!
Everyone ready?
Click
Just a moment, nearly done.

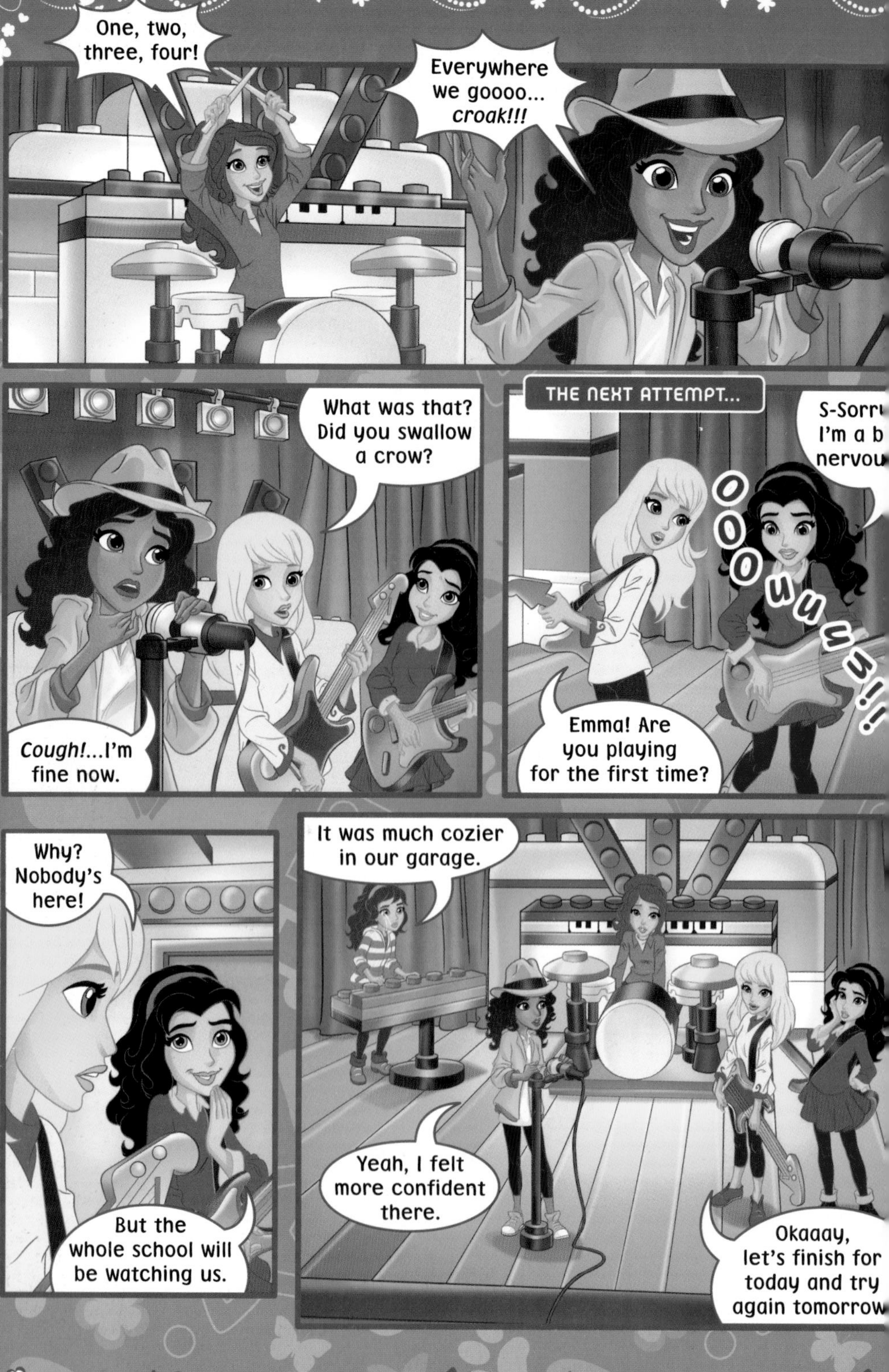
One, two, three, four!
Everywhere we goooo... *croak!!!*
What was that? Did you swallow a crow?
Cough!...I'm fine now.
THE NEXT ATTEMPT...
S-Sorr I'm a b nervou
OOOOuuuuu!!!
Emma! Are you playing for the first time?
Why? Nobody's here!
But the whole school will be watching us.
It was much cozier in our garage.
Yeah, I felt more confident there.
Okaaay, let's finish for today and try again tomorrow

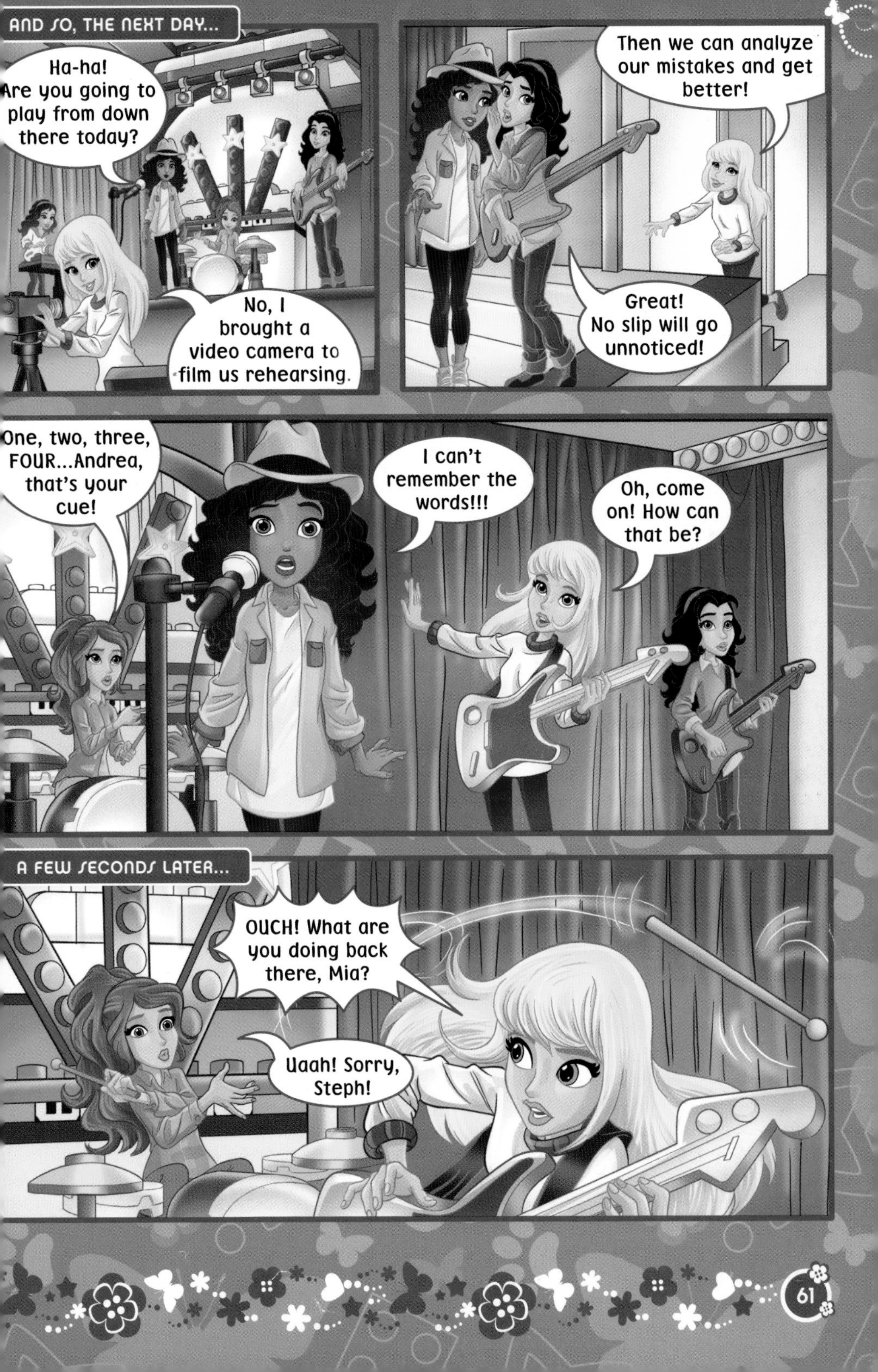
AND SO, THE NEXT DAY...
Ha-ha! Are you going to play from down there today?
No, I brought a video camera to film us rehearsing.
Then we can analyze our mistakes and get better!
Great! No slip will go unnoticed!
One, two, three, FOUR...Andrea, that's your cue!
I can't remember the words!!!
Oh, come on! How can that be?
A FEW SECONDS LATER...
OUCH! What are you doing back there, Mia?
Uaah! Sorry, Steph!

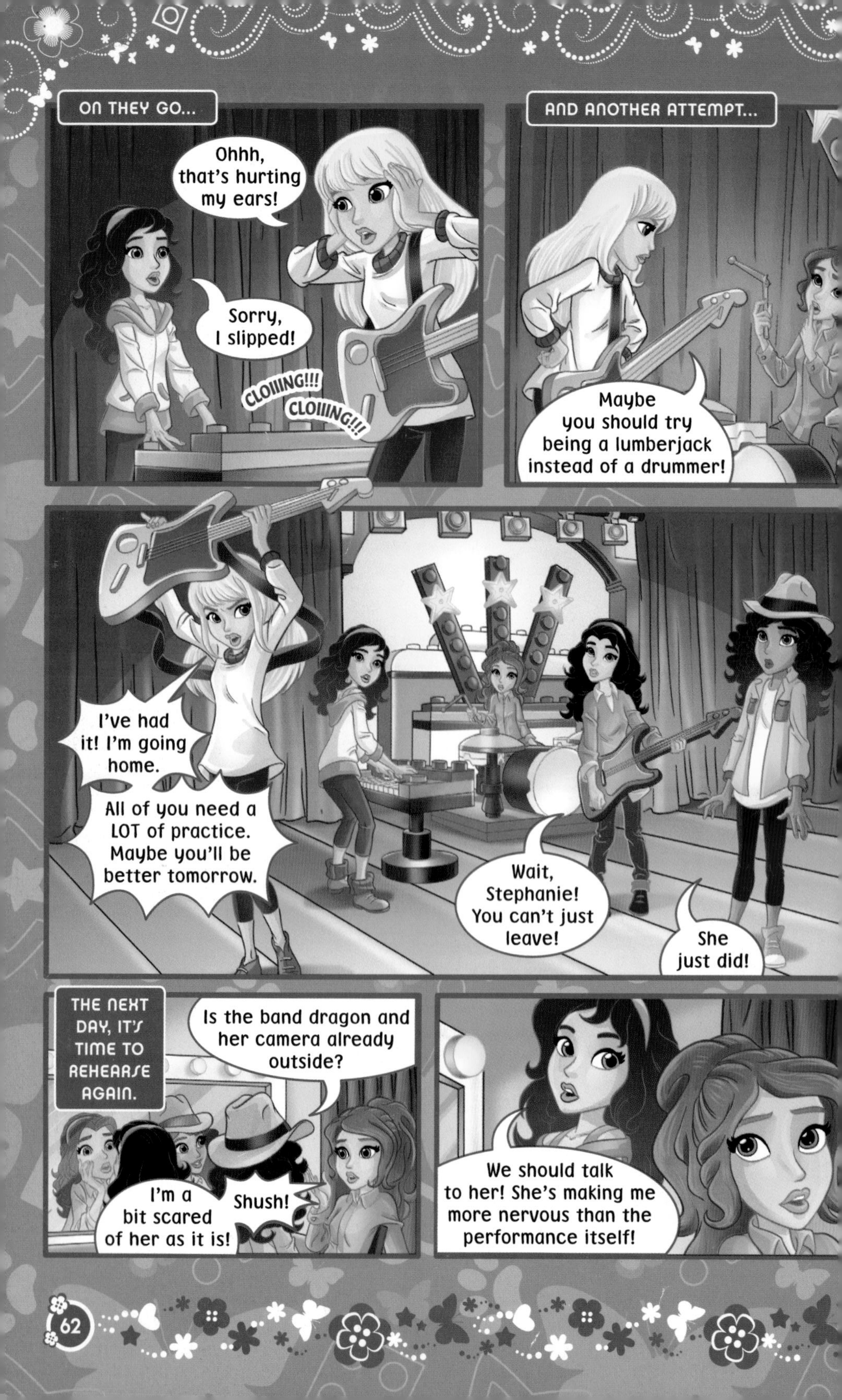
ON THEY GO...
Ohhh, that's hurting my ears!
Sorry, I slipped!
CLOIIING!!!
CLOIIING!!!
AND ANOTHER ATTEMPT...
Maybe you should try being a lumberjack instead of a drummer!
I've had it! I'm going home.
All of you need a LOT of practice. Maybe you'll be better tomorrow.
Wait, Stephanie! You can't just leave!
She just did!
THE NEXT DAY, IT'S TIME TO REHEARSE AGAIN.
Is the band dragon and her camera already outside?
I'm a bit scared of her as it is!
Shush!
We should talk to her! She's making me more nervous than the performance itself!

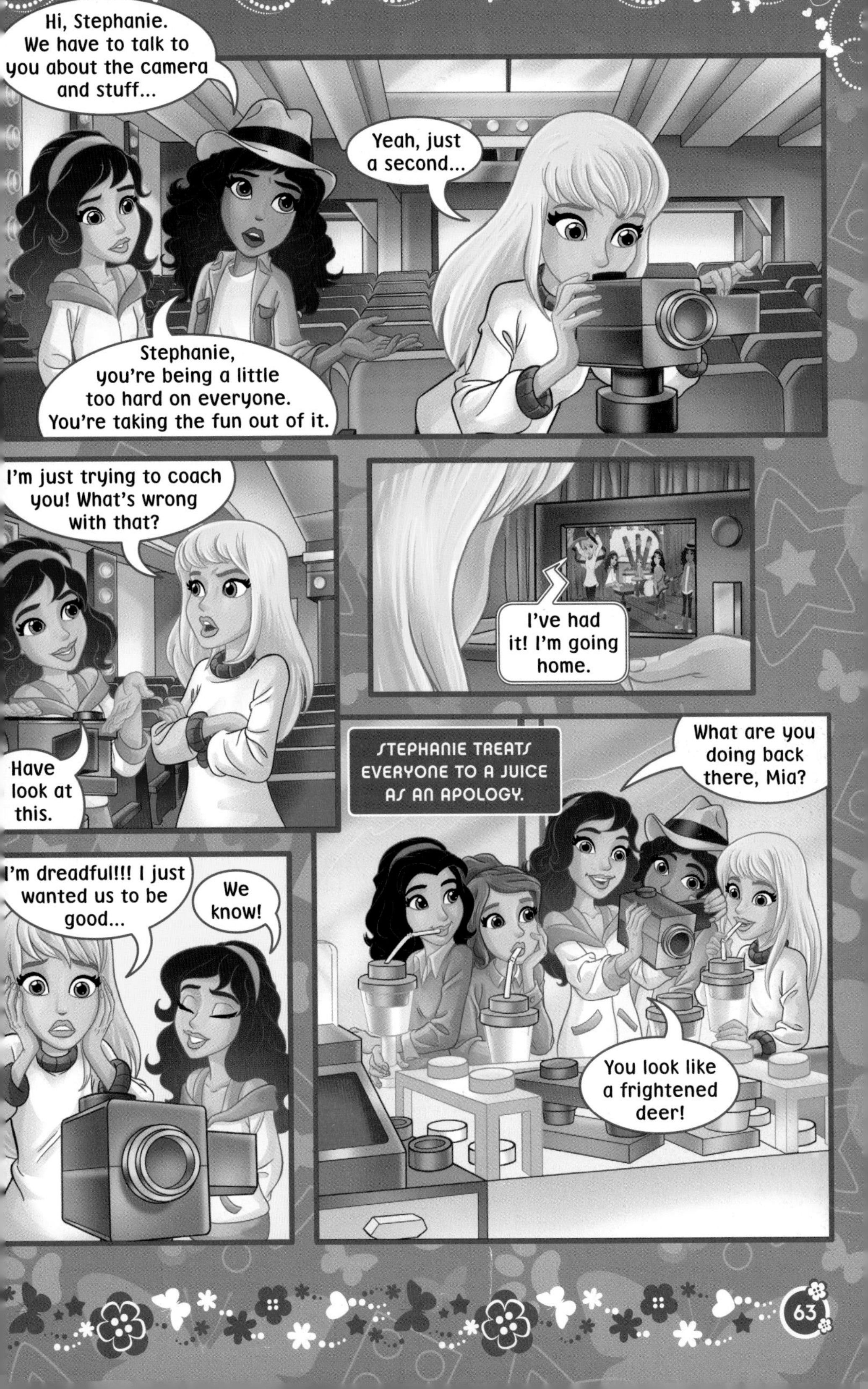
Hi, Stephanie. We have to talk to you about the camera and stuff...
Yeah, just a second...
Stephanie, you're being a little too hard on everyone. You're taking the fun out of it.
I'm just trying to coach you! What's wrong with that?
Have look at this.
I've had it! I'm going home.
STEPHANIE TREATS EVERYONE TO A JUICE AS AN APOLOGY.
What are you doing back there, Mia?
You look like a frightened deer!
I'm dreadful!!! I just wanted us to be good...
We know!

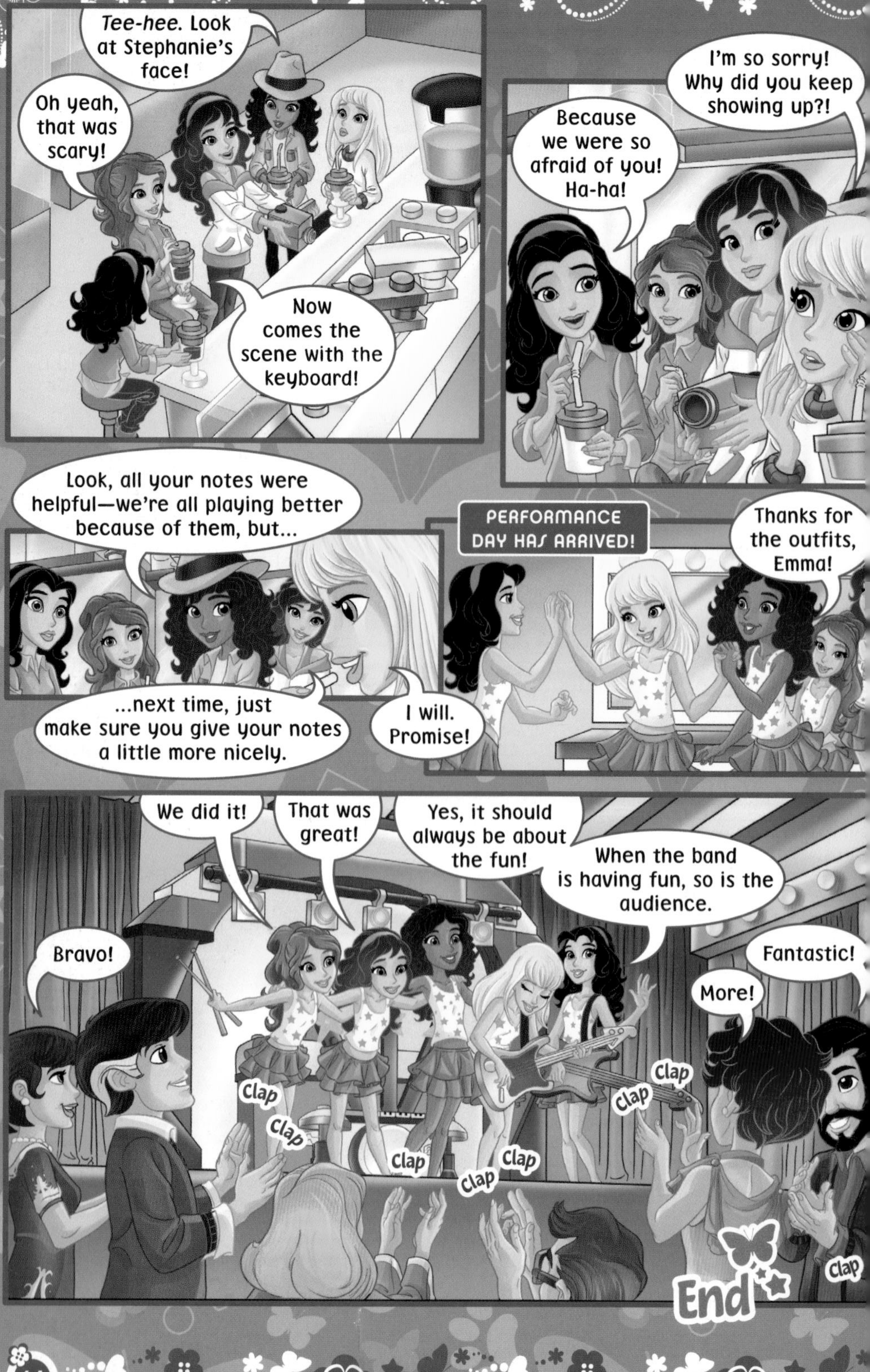
Tee-hee. Look at Stephanie's face!
Oh yeah, that was scary!
Now comes the scene with the keyboard!
I'm so sorry! Why did you keep showing up?!
Because we were so afraid of you! Ha-ha!
Look, all your notes were helpful—we're all playing better because of them, but...
...next time, just make sure you give your notes a little more nicely.
I will. Promise!
PERFORMANCE DAY HAS ARRIVED!
Thanks for the outfits, Emma!
We did it!
That was great!
Yes, it should always be about the fun!
When the band is having fun, so is the audience.
Bravo!
Fantastic!
More!
Clap
Clap
Clap
Clap
Clap
Clap
Clap
Clap
End

What's YOUR Band?

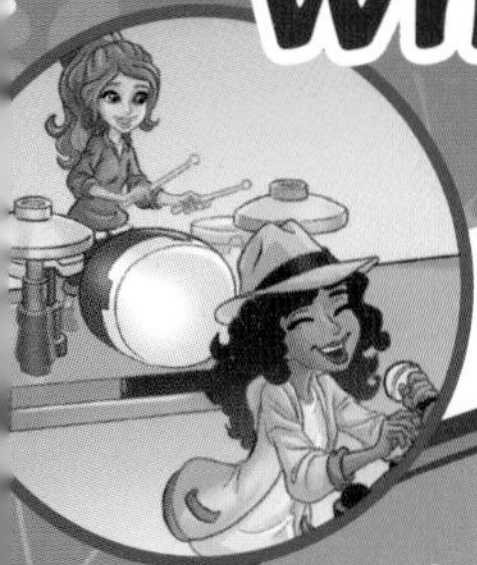

A Fun Quiz!

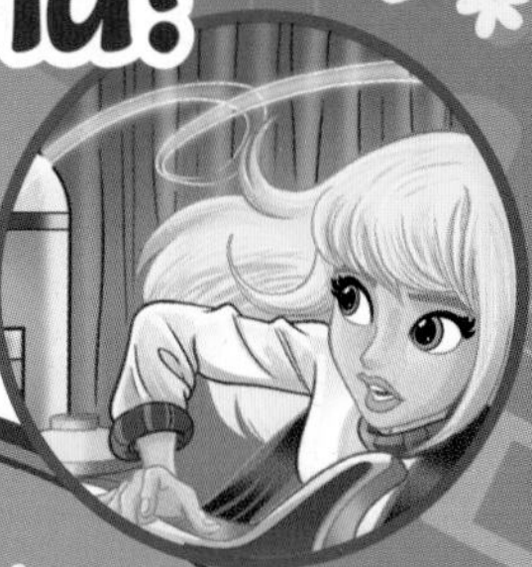

Ever wanted to be a star? Here's your chance to find out what music fits your personality! Just answer these questions and start rockin'!

1. What kind of music do you like to listen to?
   - A. Really loud with LOTS of guitar—who needs to hear the words?
   - B. Pretty lyrics, soft melody
   - C. Something I can dance to!

2. How would you name your band?
   - A. Take two crazy words and put them together
   - B. Choose something that inspires me
   - C. After me, obviously!

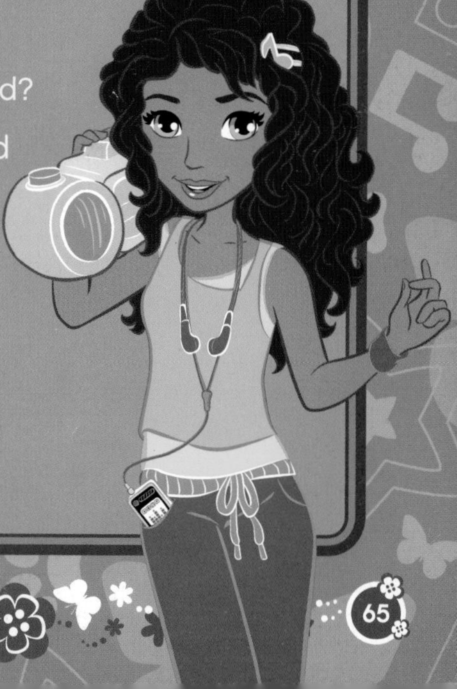

3. What would one of your concerts be like?

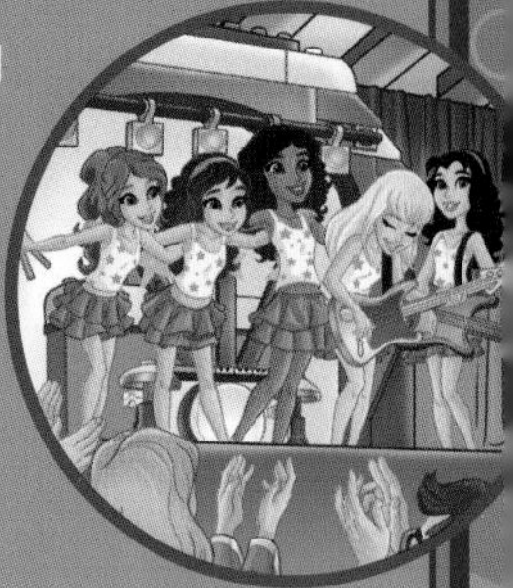

   A. There would be a lot of screaming fans bumping into one another.
   B. It would be in a small café with just me and my fans.
   C. It would be a huge performance with dance routines and costumes!

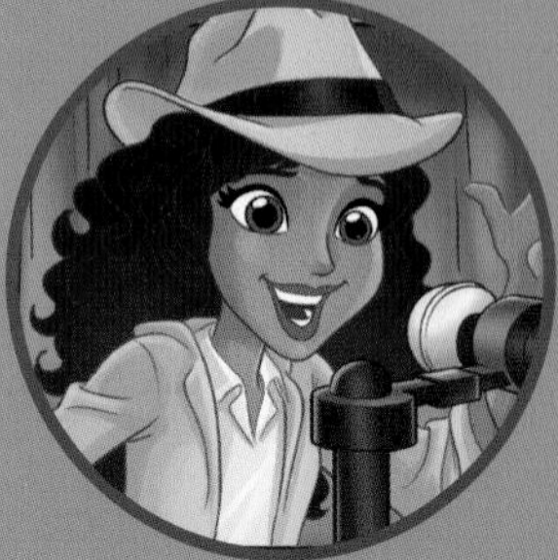

4. What instrument do you play?
   A. Electric guitar or drums
   B. Acoustic guitar and vocals
   C. Just my voice!

ANSWERS:

A's: If you chose mostly A's, you're in a serious rock or metal band. You like loud music, screaming lyrics, and hyper fans!

B's: If you chose mostly B's, you're in a folk rock band. You like smaller shows, soulful lyrics, and fans who like to listen.

C's: If you chose mostly C's, you're a pop star all the way! You love putting on a show and being at the center of it.

A Difficult Decision

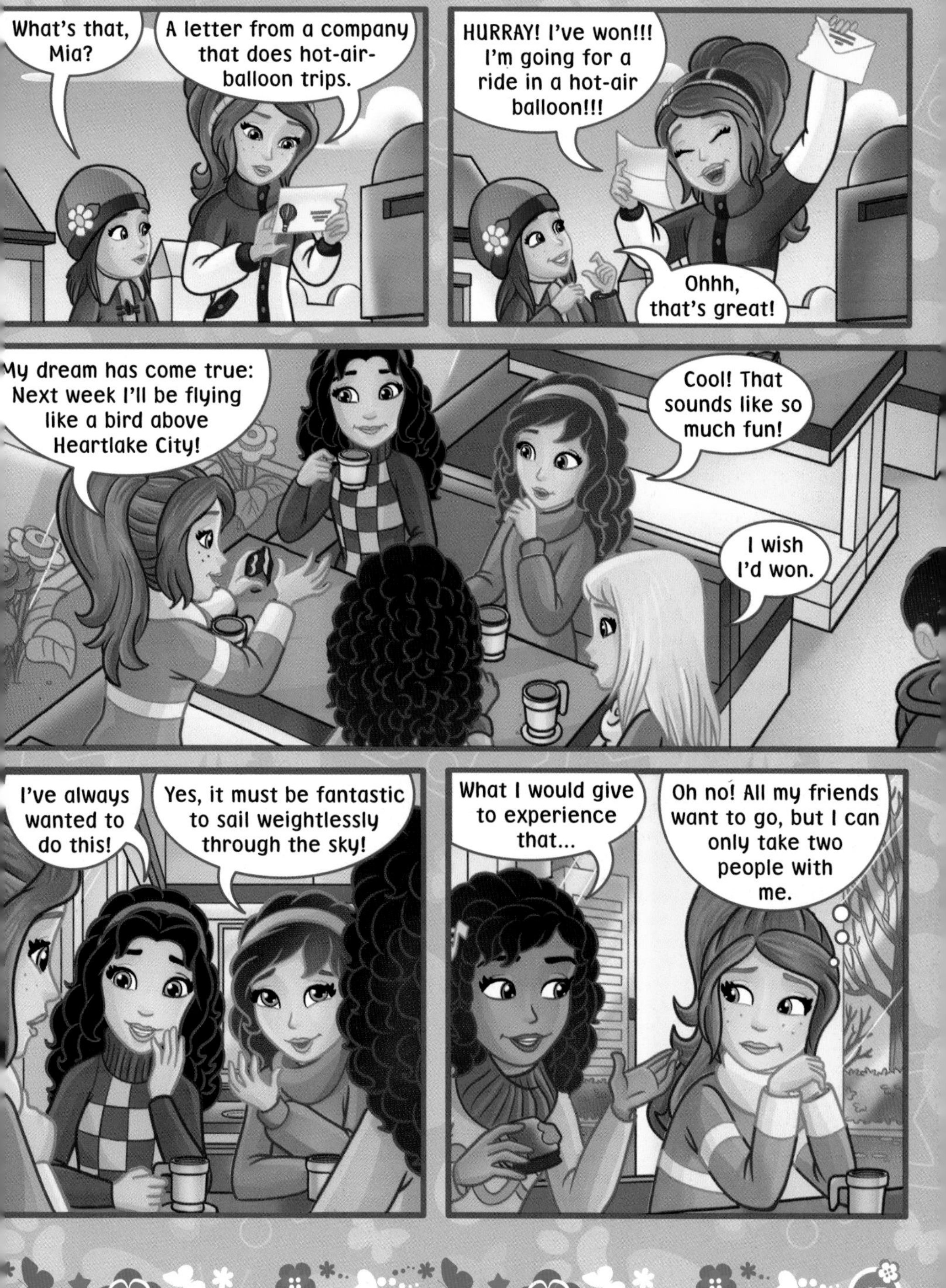
What's that, Mia?
A letter from a company that does hot-air-balloon trips.
HURRAY! I've won!!! I'm going for a ride in a hot-air balloon!!!
Ohhh, that's great!
My dream has come true: Next week I'll be flying like a bird above Heartlake City!
Cool! That sounds like so much fun!
I wish I'd won.
I've always wanted to do this!
Yes, it must be fantastic to sail weightlessly through the sky!
What I would give to experience that...
Oh no! All my friends want to go, but I can only take two people with me.

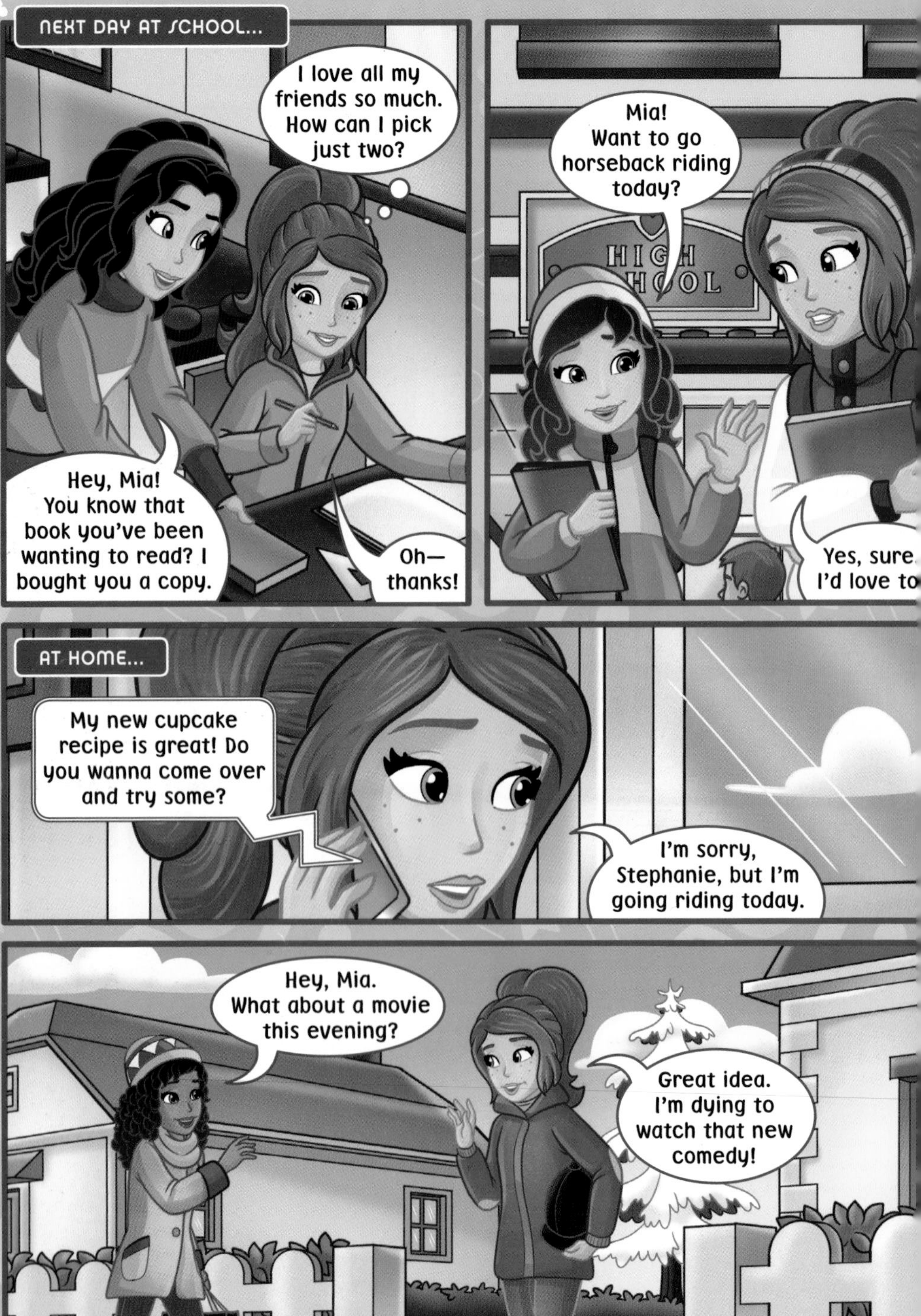
NEXT DAY AT SCHOOL...
I love all my friends so much. How can I pick just two?
Hey, Mia! You know that book you've been wanting to read? I bought you a copy.
Oh— thanks!
Mia! Want to go horseback riding today?
HIGH SCHOOL
Yes, sure. I'd love to
AT HOME...
My new cupcake recipe is great! Do you wanna come over and try some?
I'm sorry, Stephanie, but I'm going riding today.
Hey, Mia. What about a movie this evening?
Great idea. I'm dying to watch that new comedy!

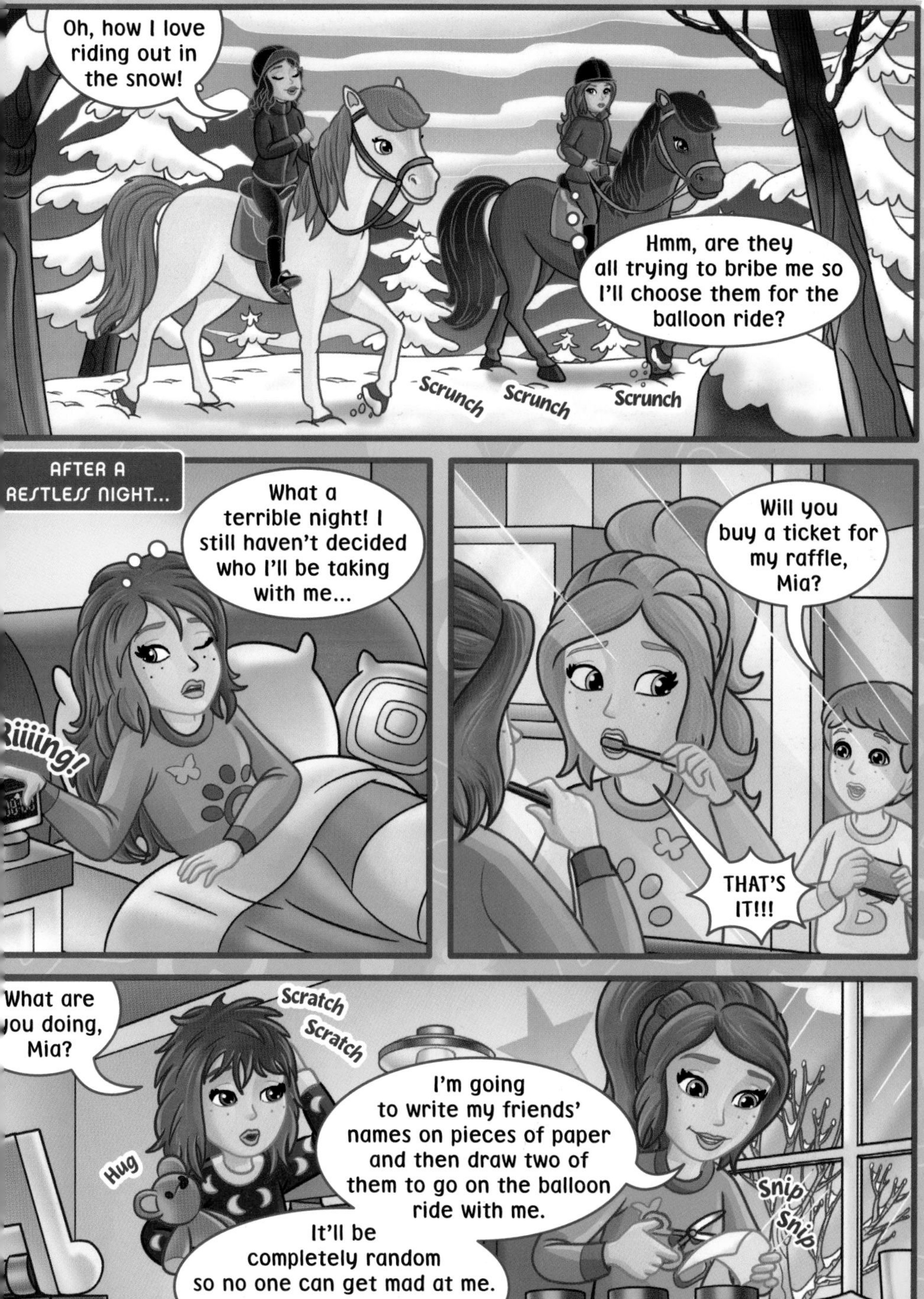
Oh, how I love riding out in the snow!
Hmm, are they all trying to bribe me so I'll choose them for the balloon ride?
Scrunch
Scrunch
Scrunch
AFTER A RESTLESS NIGHT...
What a terrible night! I still haven't decided who I'll be taking with me...
Riiiing!
Will you buy a ticket for my raffle, Mia?
THAT'S IT!!!
What are you doing, Mia?
Scratch
Scratch
Hug
I'm going to write my friends' names on pieces of paper and then draw two of them to go on the balloon ride with me.
It'll be completely random so no one can get mad at me.
Snip
Snip

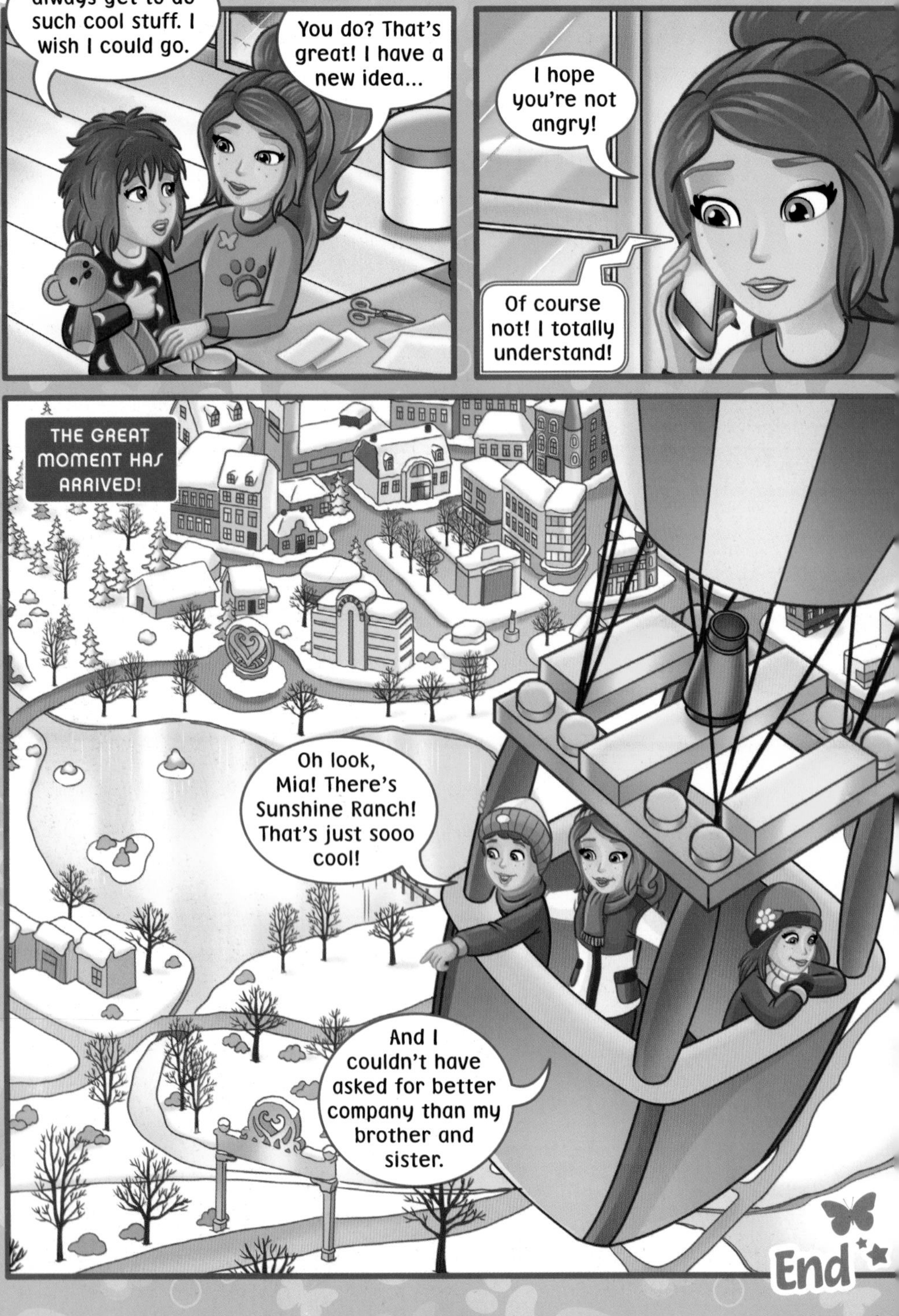
You big kids always get to do such cool stuff. I wish I could go.
You do? That's great! I have a new idea...
I hope you're not angry!
Of course not! I totally understand!
THE GREAT MOMENT HAS ARRIVED!
Oh look, Mia! There's Sunshine Ranch! That's just sooo cool!
And I couldn't have asked for better company than my brother and sister.
End

Decisions, Decisions

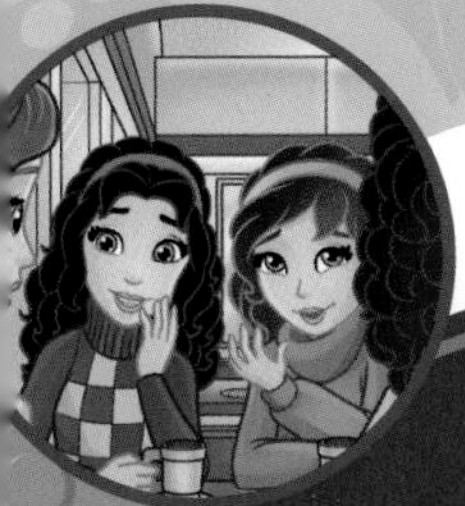

A Bit of Advice

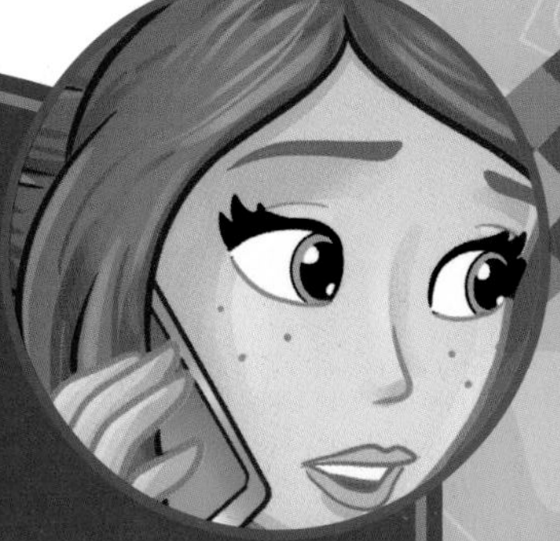

Have you ever had to make a hard decision like Mia did in this story? Who should you invite to your birthday party? Should you use your allowance to buy an expensive item, or should you save your money? Would it be more fun to spend the weekend at the beach or at an amusement park?

Decisions can be tricky, and sometimes it's hard to know if you're making the right one. It's especially hard when your friends are involved and you don't want to hurt someone's feelings. Here are some things you can do to help yourself in difficult situations.

Ask Someone You Trust

If you're having trouble making a decision, get another perspective. Asking for help is always a good plan when you have to make an important decision. Parents and grandparents are usually the best people to ask. They have a lot of "life experience," and they'll have your best interests in mind when they consider your decision.

This person could also be an older sibling, a good friend, or even a teacher. Any of these people probably won't tell you exactly what to do, but they'll help guide you toward the best decision for *you*—because they know you so well!

Make a List of Pros and Cons

Divide a piece of paper into two even sections. On one side, write down all the positive things about your decision. On the other side, write down all the negative things about making that same decision. Then compare your lists to see which is longer. If something has more negatives than positives, avoid it! You can do this for all the options you have until you find the best answer to your problem.

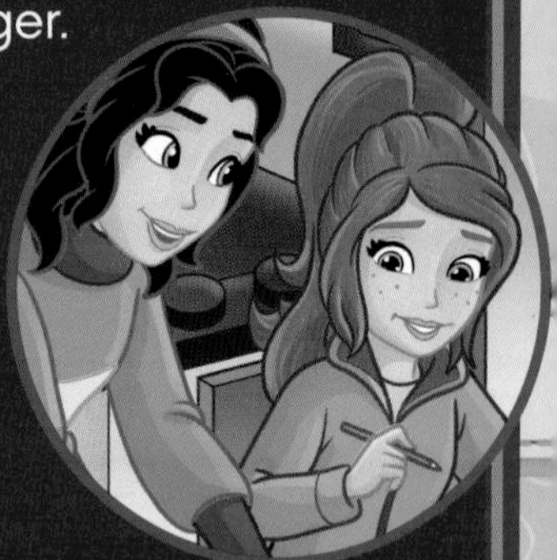

Research

Another great method for making a decision is investigating your options. For instance, if you can't decide between going to the beach or going to an amusement park, learn more about both places. You should consider things like cost, travel, and of course, what sounds more fun to you. After educating yourself about your decision, it usually becomes much easier to decide.

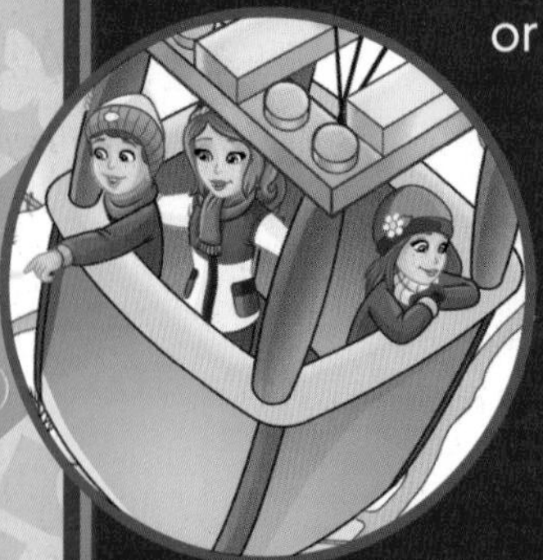

Nothing but Riding on Her Mind!

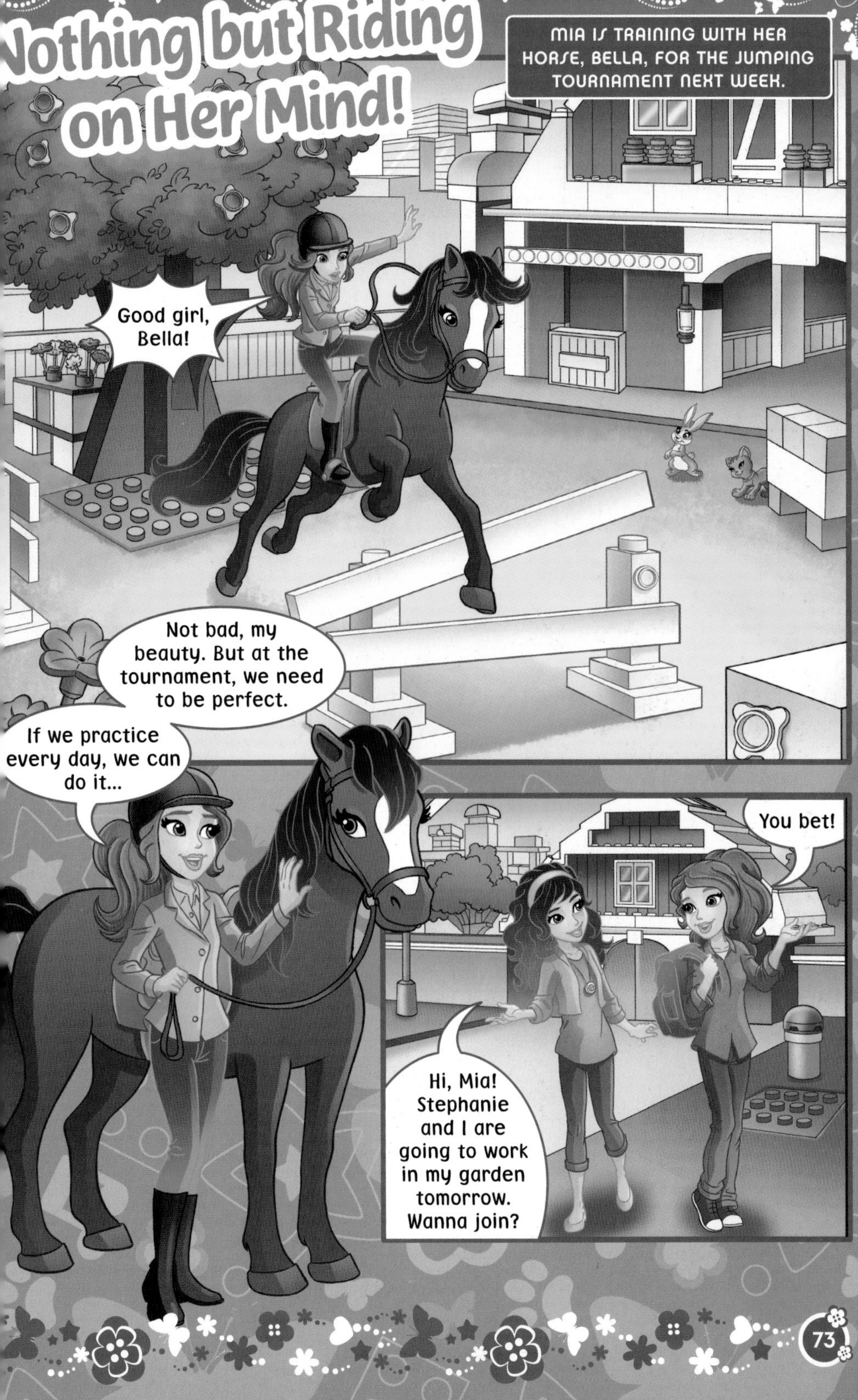
MIA IS TRAINING WITH HER HORSE, BELLA, FOR THE JUMPING TOURNAMENT NEXT WEEK.
Good girl, Bella!
Not bad, my beauty. But at the tournament, we need to be perfect.
If we practice every day, we can do it...
Hi, Mia! Stephanie and I are going to work in my garden tomorrow. Wanna join?
You bet!

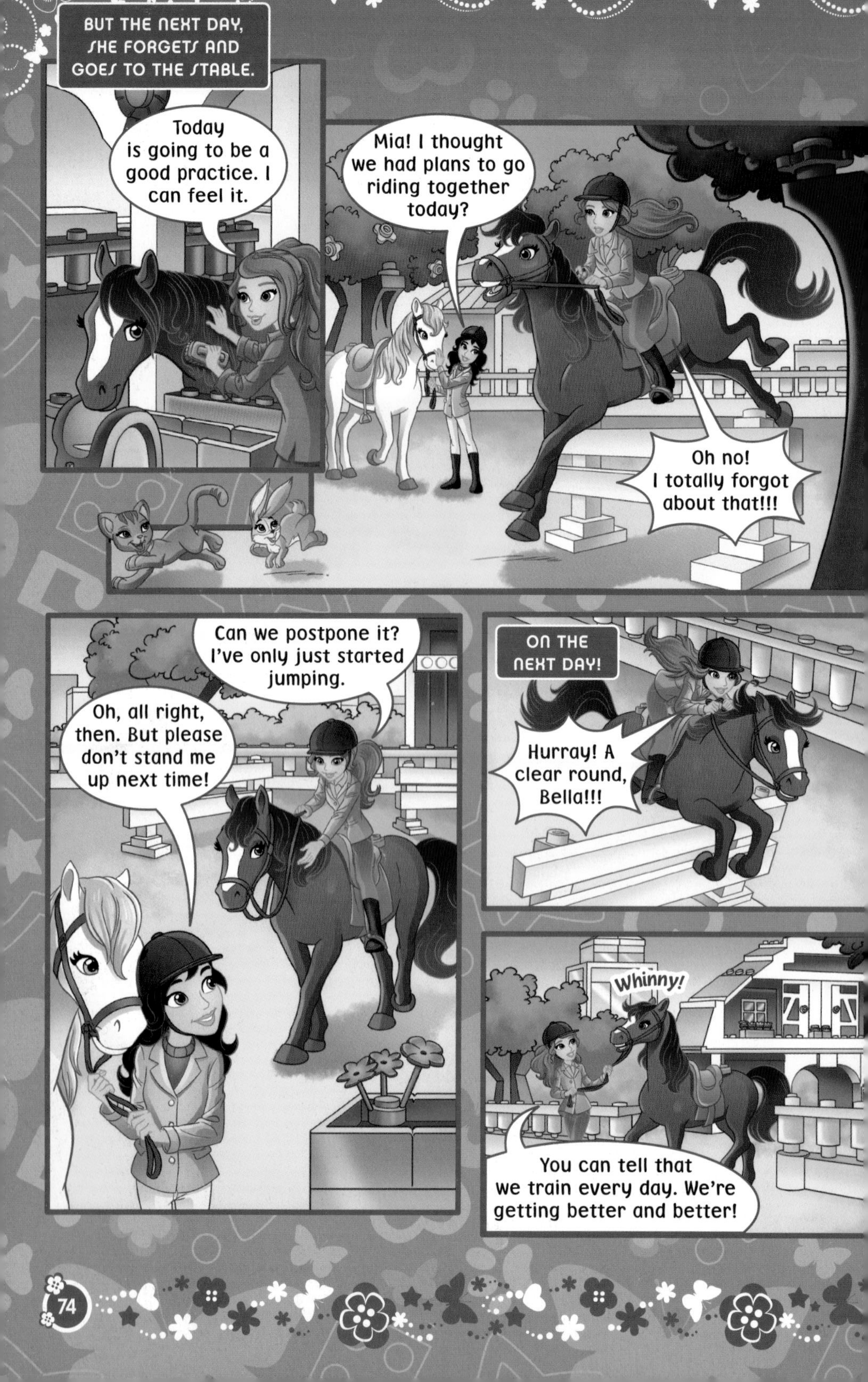
BUT THE NEXT DAY, SHE FORGETS AND GOES TO THE STABLE.
Today is going to be a good practice. I can feel it.
Mia! I thought we had plans to go riding together today?
Oh no! I totally forgot about that!!!
Can we postpone it? I've only just started jumping.
Oh, all right, then. But please don't stand me up next time!
ON THE NEXT DAY!
Hurray! A clear round, Bella!!!
Whinny!
You can tell that we train every day. We're getting better and better!

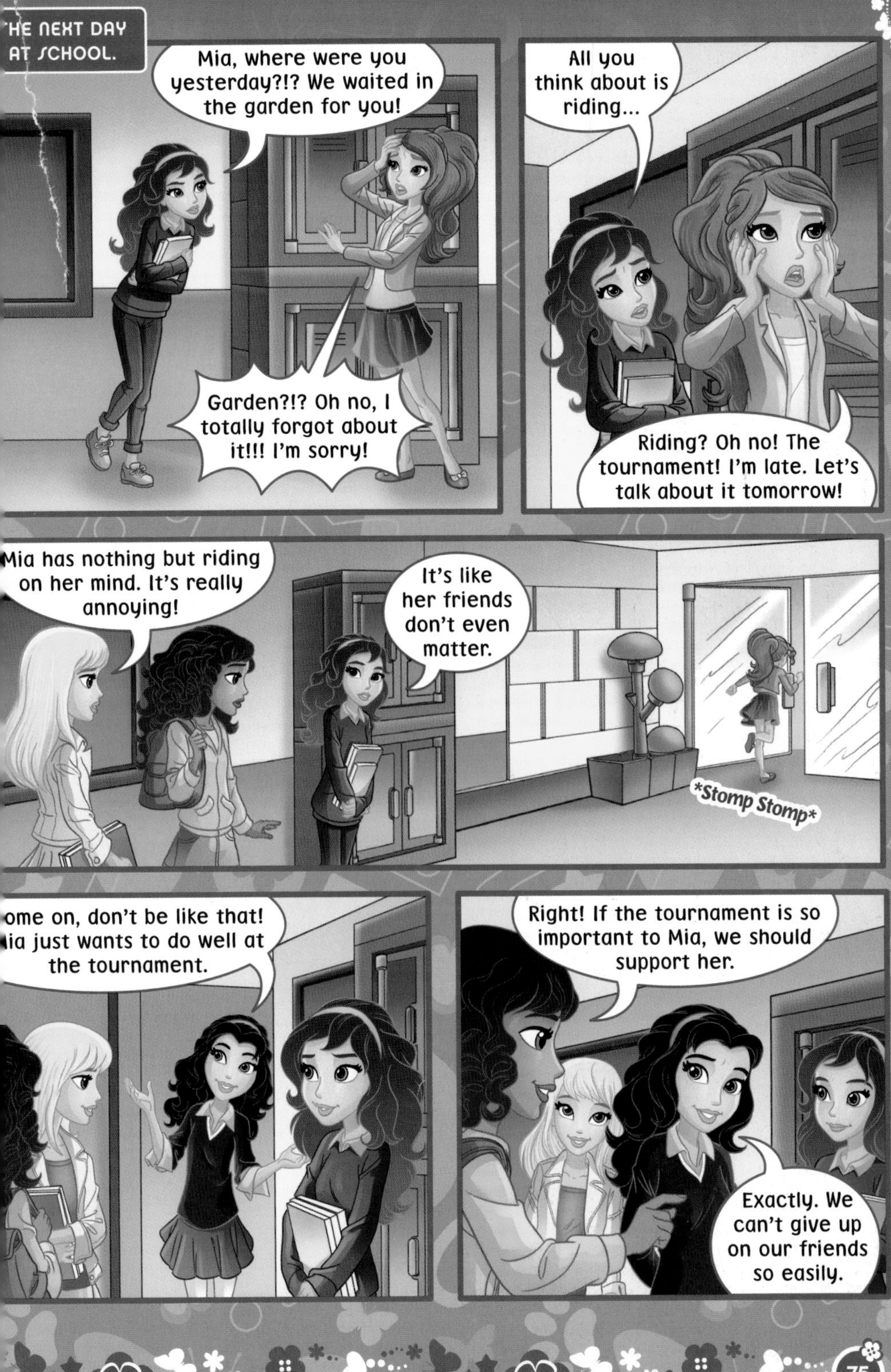
HE NEXT DAY AT SCHOOL.
Mia, where were you yesterday?!? We waited in the garden for you!
Garden?!? Oh no, I totally forgot about it!!! I'm sorry!
All you think about is riding...
Riding? Oh no! The tournament! I'm late. Let's talk about it tomorrow!
Mia has nothing but riding on her mind. It's really annoying!
It's like her friends don't even matter.
Stomp Stomp
ome on, don't be like that! ia just wants to do well at the tournament.
Right! If the tournament is so important to Mia, we should support her.
Exactly. We can't give up on our friends so easily.

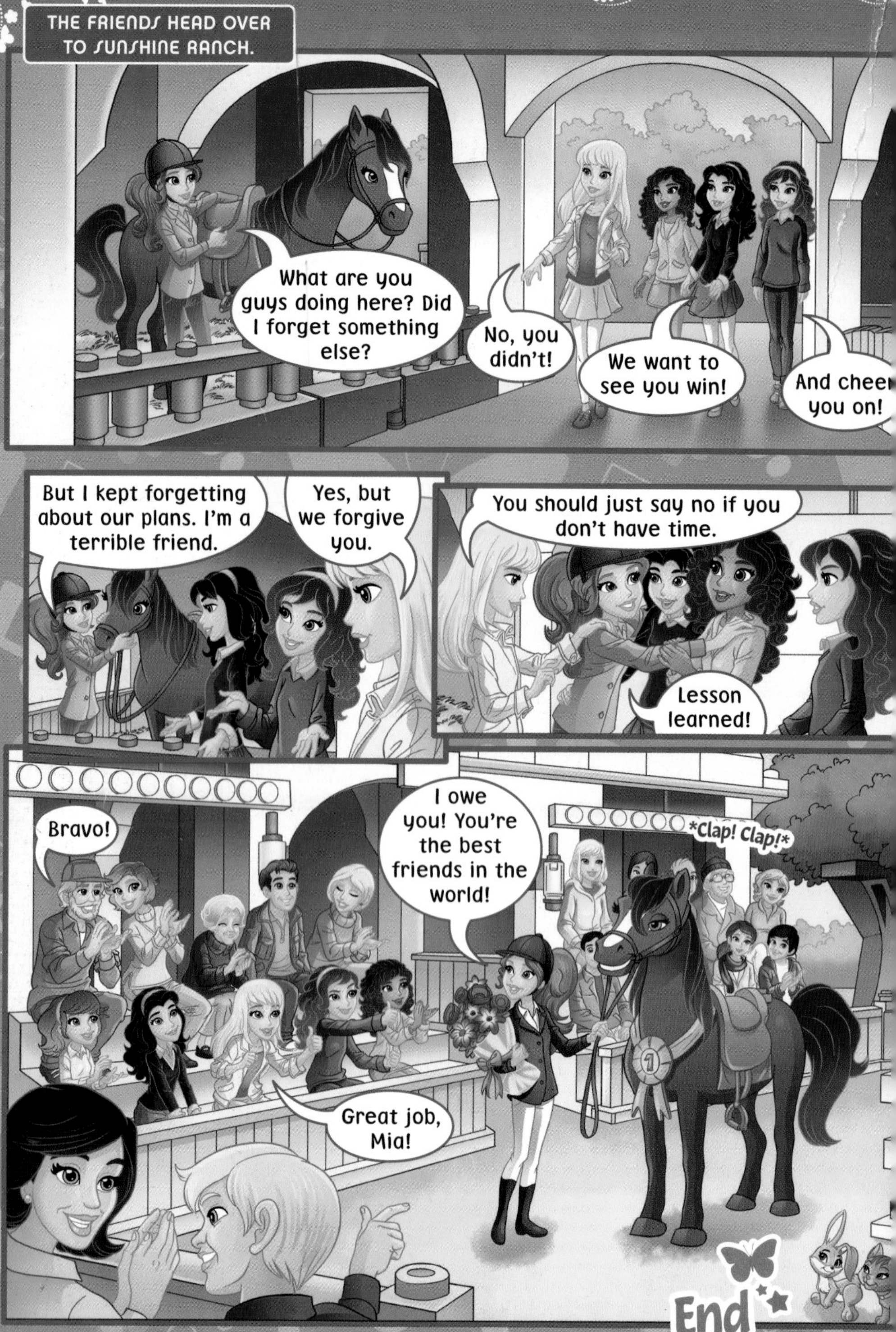
THE FRIENDS HEAD OVER TO SUNSHINE RANCH.
What are you guys doing here? Did I forget something else?
No, you didn't!
We want to see you win!
And cheer you on!
But I kept forgetting about our plans. I'm a terrible friend.
Yes, but we forgive you.
You should just say no if you don't have time.
Lesson learned!
Bravo!
I owe you! You're the best friends in the world!
Clap! Clap!
Great job, Mia!
End

Friends Forever

More Advice

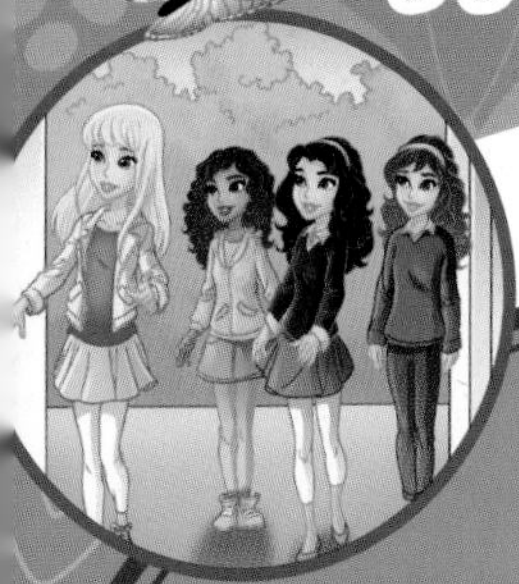

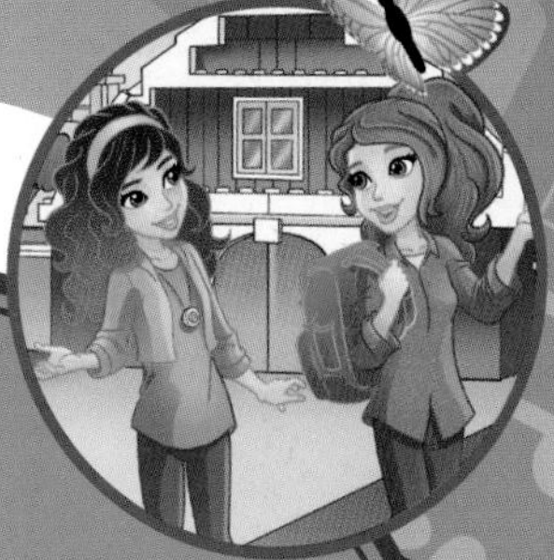

Friends are some of the most important people in our lives. They know our deepest secrets, share in our celebrations, and are there for us when we're sad. But did you know that keeping a friendship in good shape takes some work? Every friendship needs to be given attention, care, and love for it to grow strong and last forever. If you and one of your friends get into a fight, or you just want to strengthen the bonds you already have, these creative activities are great ways to strengthen your friendship bond!

Write a Note

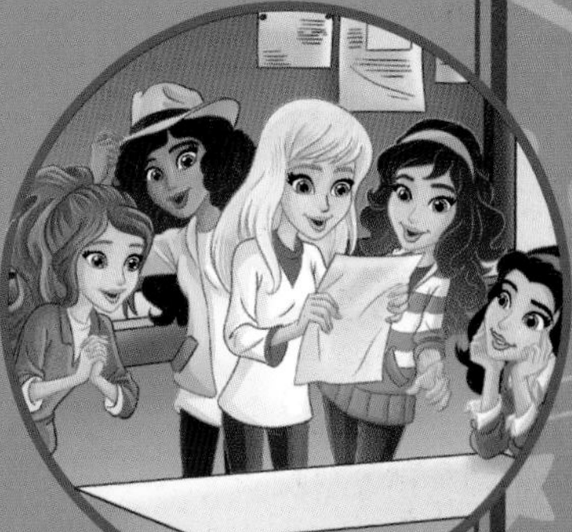

Write your friend a note telling her something about her that you love. It could be about how funny she is, or how she always lets you borrow her clothes, or even how much she knows about math! Have her do the same for you and then exchange them!

Share a Good and Bad Moment

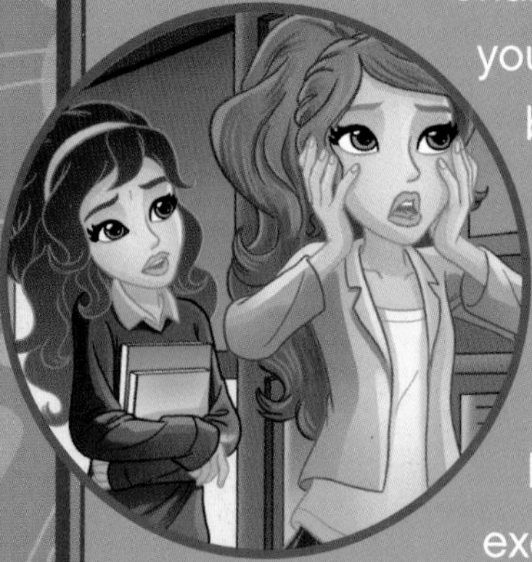

Share a time when your friend helped you with a problem or made you feel better about something when you were sad. Tell her how much this meant to you. Then share a time when you might have been hurt by something she did and explain to her why. Have her do the same. This exercise will help you appreciate the good times and help you learn from your mistakes so you become the best friends you can be!

Just the Two of You

Take some time to plan a special activity to share together. This could be making each other matching friendship bracelets, going to a movie or concert together, or having a friendship slumber party! Just choose something to celebrate how wonderful your friendship is and how happy you are to have found each other.

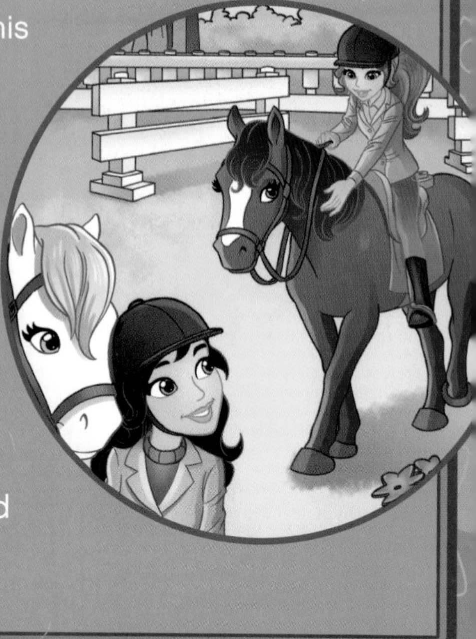

Make a Friendship Album

Put together a photo album of your friendship. Use as many pictures as you can find from the time your friendship began until now, and write down where you were, what you were doing, and when each picture was taken. Be sure to include silly stories, too. You can make one album to share, or you can make two different ones so you can each have one to keep!

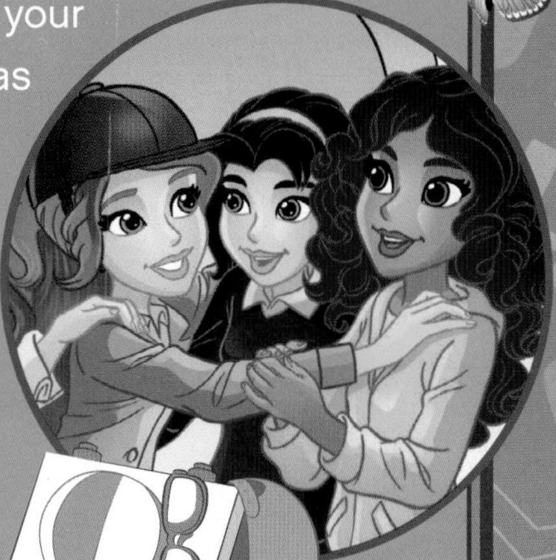

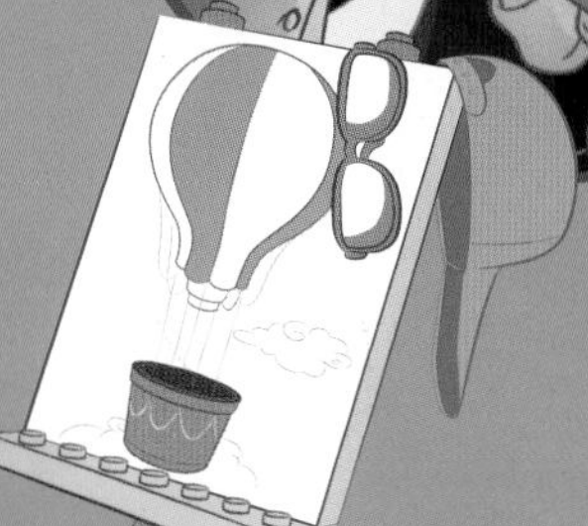

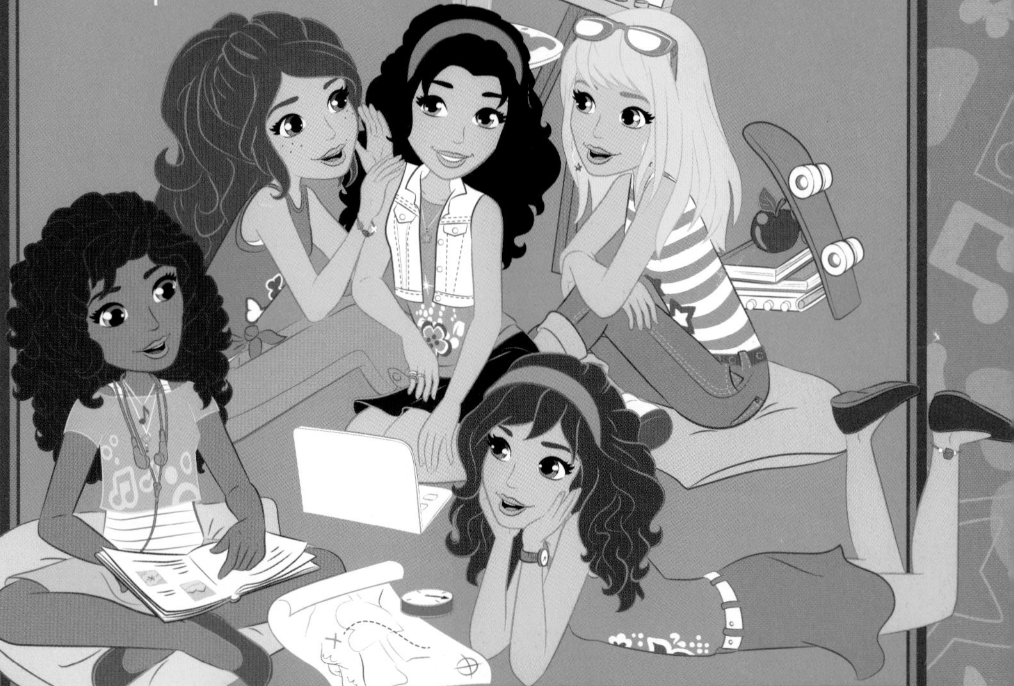

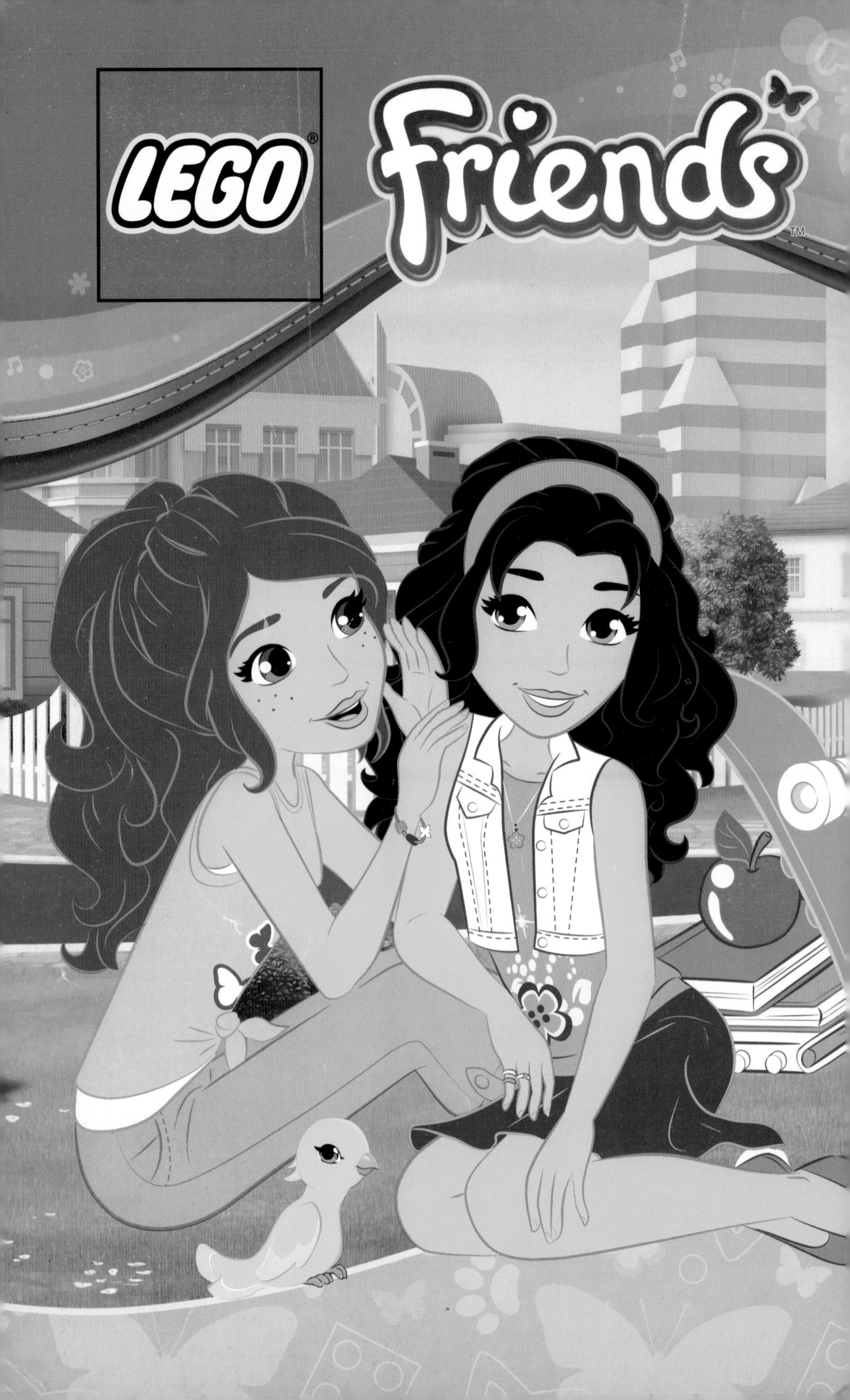
LEGO
friends